# KEY OF POWER

NANCY GOLDEN

GOLDEN CROSS RANCH LLC

For information or inquiries, email Nancy Golden at
nancy@goldencrossranch.com

Library of Congress Control Number: 2025903070

Published by Golden Cross Ranch LLC
Carrollton, Texas U.S.A.

Cover Design by Piere d' Arterie
https://99designs.com/profiles/pieredarterie

*To my big brother and forever friend,*
*Eddie Venetucci.*
*Having a brother is wonderful! It means always having someone cheering you on and being understood and loved for all eternity. Eddie, your love and care for our family and your compassion and nurturing nature for others is a blessing and an inspiration for all of us. I am so grateful God picked me to be your baby sister. You'll always be my Maytag repairman. Much love always.*

*And to Eddie's beloved wife, my sister-in-law, Susan Venetucci. She has such a sweet and loving spirit and is the sister of my heart.*

# JUST A QUICK NOTE TO MY READERS

I am so excited about Key of Power for many different reasons. The book was very fun to write! All of our old friends, both human and magical creatures, are back—as well as many new ones. In this final book of the *Dynamis* Series Trilogy, the ultimate battle of good versus evil takes place. Think about what you are reading on the surface as a fun and exciting adventure, but don't forget to dig a little deeper. As is true of most stories, Key of Power has multiple layers of meaning. Nuggets of treasure are there waiting for you to find them! It is my hope that your journey through Key of Power serves to inspire you in many different ways.

I also want to encourage you to wonder about the world around you. Take inspiration from the things that you read and learn about. One of the magical devices that I use in writing this book was inspired by something I ran across on the internet that has been attributed to Archimedes. I found a painting regarding it that really stirred my imagination (I kept it as my screensaver for a few weeks to inspire me) and you will see the impact that it had on me in the pages of this story. Because the picture is in the public domain, I was able to include it in the back of the book.

You never know what will serve to cause you to think of something you might not have thought about before or to have a fresh realization on a familiar topic. Try to get rid of your earbuds once in a while and use all of your five senses whether you are inside or outside. You may be reading a book, taking a walk, shopping, or at a museum. Stay alert and open to new opportunities and new revelations. Be aware of your surroundings. The world is a wonderful place, and you don't want to miss out on something special that could be right in front of you!

For those of you who have read books one and two in the *Dynamis* series, I am so excited that you are joining me for the culmination of Rugal's story (and of course his companions) in book three. There may be other books in the future around this wonderful fantasy world that we have built together, but this is the completion of the stories revolving around each of the three symbols that designate Rugal as the true King of Elayas. The characters and their relationships and how they have moved through a constantly changing world together mean so much to me and I hope they have touched your heart as much as they have mine.

Now, get ready to experience this final climactic battle between good and evil. Read with an open mind and an open heart and enjoy the journey!

*My wish for you is to ride dragons and leviathans often and to have your own flutebird—never stop reading! The places you go in your imagination to relax and to refresh will energize you and help you face the battles of real life with a positive mindset. There is enough trouble in the world—read books that you find inspiring and uplifting. And always remember the Kargolith proverb: Dark-ness may descend, but light shall overcome it.*

*Much Love,*
*Nancy Golden*

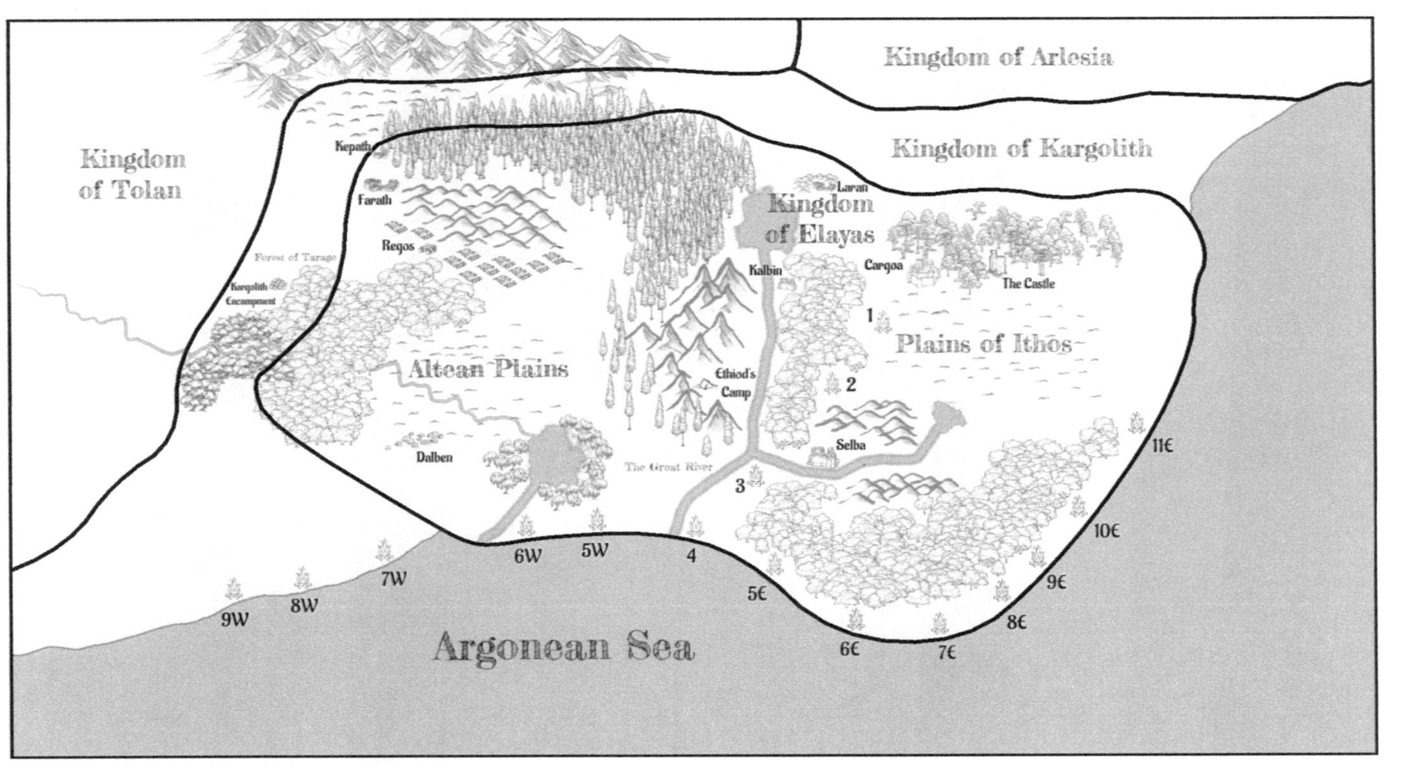

Kingdom of Arlesia
Kingdom of Kargolith
Kingdom of Tolan
Kingdom of Elayas
Laran
Cargoa
The Castle
Plains of Ithos
Kepath
Farath
Reqos
Forest of Tarago
Kargolith Encampment
Kalbin
Altean Plains
Ethiod's Camp
Selba
Dalben
The Great River
1
2
3
4
5E
6E
7E
8E
9E
10E
11E
4W
5W
6W
7W
8W
9W
Argonean Sea

# PROLOGUE

An oracle from the Ring of Rosin prophesied that the Neliphim, a force of great evil, would come from across the sea at the end of winter to destroy Elayas, Tolan, and Kargolith. Now, the end of winter is approaching...

King Rugal asked the Ring of Rosin:

"How can we stop them?"

The oracle answered:

*"Your futures are dependent on your kingdoms working together. You, Johan, and Hamideh are marked, and each of you will have to give up something you hold dear for the greater good. Even so, there are no assurances. The future is cloudy."*

# CHAPTER
# ONE

"Without a vision, there is no future."
~ Tanan, philosopher of Selba

Finn peered through the trees surrounding the manicured lawn of the castle. She had tucked her bright red hair into a cap to avoid being spotted as she scouted the castle grounds. With a hopeful expression, she scanned the area that contained the practice yard. Surely, the Swordsman would make an appearance soon. If only she could catch him alone. She couldn't trust anyone else, and she didn't know where else to turn.

A movement caught her attention, and she let out a frustrated sigh. For the third morning in a row, the Swordsman appeared, and someone approached him almost immediately from the castle environs. The chance for a private meeting was gone yet again. Finn wiped a grimy hand across her face, rubbing away the single tear that had trickled down her cheek.

Noting the morning sun had risen higher in the sky, she melted back into the forest. She would need to find something to eat and a place to sleep undetected until she could try again.

RUGAL DREW the Sword of Fate and grinned at the man towering before him. "What say you, Swordsman? Have you time for a practice session?"

The Swordsman smiled affectionately at the young king. "Of course, Sire, it would be my pleasure." He drew his own sword and awaited Rugal's thrust.

Rugal lunged forward, the blue stone on the crosspiece of his sword flashing in the sunlight. The two swords clashed midair, steel upon steel, as the two combatants danced around the practice yard.

"You have been practicing the Dalbenian bluff," the Swordsman observed. "Well done, young Rugal."

Rugal beamed under the Swordsman's praise as he wiped the sweat from his brow. "I have. It's been a difficult maneuver for me, but I think I have finally mastered it." His expression changed, and his brow creased with concern. "I may have need of it once we begin our campaign against the Neliphim."

"Let us hope you never have to get that close," the Swordsman responded. Before he could comment further, a dark shadow passed overhead.

Rugal looked skyward with happy anticipation. Argothal was backwinging onto the castle courtyard, with Johan and Hamideh astride the giant beast. Having a dragon for a friend was an honor, and also very handy. He was grateful that the fierce dragon was willing to transport the leader of the Kargoliths and the King of Tolan.

He glanced at the Swordsman, who nodded and gestured toward the dragon. "Your friends will be glad to see you."

Rugal sheathed his sword and strode toward the courtyard. A flash of feathers flew by his head, accompanied by a happy trilling noise, as Treble quickly winged past to greet Argothal.

Rugal gave Argothal an affectionate scratch on his lowered head as Johan then Hamideh stepped onto Argothal's proffered foreleg and leapt to the ground, their faces flushed with excitement.

Johan and Hamideh clasped Rugal's extended hand, and all three shouted in unison, "Never pass up the opportunity to ride a dragon!" dissolving in laughter as Argothal craned his neck and regarded them with a curious expression.

Catching their breaths, the three faced the dragon, and their expressions turned serious.

"Thank you, Argothal. We are grateful for your service to Elayas," Rugal formally expressed their gratitude. Treble added a melodious note in emphasis, and all three broke into smiles again. Argothal dipped his head in acknowledgment.

Mura looked out the window. Her eyes sparkling, she tugged at Jackal's arm. "Come to the window, my love, you must see this." The two stood side by side, peering down at the courtyard.

"I have never seen a dragon playing tag before," murmured Mura.

Jackal shook his head and chuckled. "Rugal and his friends never cease to amaze me as to what they are capable of." He gazed at his beloved. "I'll take it for a good omen. We need all the ones we can get. The end of winter will be here before we know it."

Mura's light mood disappeared at the reminder. She continued to gaze down at her son and his companions. "I am going to choose to believe they each have a great future. To think otherwise would be to admit defeat before we even get started."

Jackal slipped his arm around Mura and squeezed her shoulders. "I will join you in that belief."

"So, tell me Hamideh, now that it has been a month since your coronation, how does it feel to be king?" Rugal pitched a rock into the stream. The three young men had waved goodbye as Argothal winged his way back toward his cave in the mountains and then they wandered to a nearby meadow.

Hamideh's eyes glowed, and he licked his lips. "It is the most exhilarating and scariest experience of my life." He paused, making eye contact with Johan who nodded understandingly, then back to Rugal. "Having the responsibility for the safety and care of my people feels overwhelming at times. How can I, a mere man, provide for them and meet their needs?" He swept his unruly hair out of his eyes. "But on the other hand, having the power to govern my kingdom in the direction I believe is best for my country..." he paused and looked down, trying to find the words.

Rugal strode over to him and put a hand on his shoulder. "I understand, Hamideh. The opportunity we have been given to lead our countries is both exciting and scary. It is an awesome responsibility."

Johan moved closer, nodding in agreement. "Sometimes I wish I could go back to hunting and fishing, without having to worry about anything else." He rubbed his cheek. "But the feeling passes, and another one takes its place when I think about all the good I can do for my people." He glanced thoughtfully at his friends. "If I can find a way to protect them from harm, I will have lived out my purpose."

"A good reminder," Rugal frowned, his body stiffening, "and the reason I requested your presence. As much as I enjoy your companionship, we have a more important obligation." He pointed to one of the areas that had been cleared and set up as a fire pit, wood stacked neatly nearby. Large logs lay scattered about to provide seating. "Let's set up there. It will give us a good measure of privacy." He glanced at the position of the sun. "I can ask Lissa to have some lunch sent."

"That's right!" Hamideh bounced on his toes, and his boyish grin returned. "How wonderful to have instant communication with your betrothed, no matter how far apart you are!"

Rugal pulled at his shirt, his face flushing. Any thought of Lissa brought a flood of emotions. He wondered for what must have been the millionth time how he was so lucky to have met Ethiod Stargazer's beautiful daughter and that they had pledged their love for each other. One of the happiest days of his life was when he proposed, and she said yes.

"It is very comforting to know she is only a thought away." He smiled, his eyes gleaming with delight. "She is genuinely special, and her *dynamis* is extraordinary."

*Are you talking about me?*

Rugal jumped, the sweet and playful lilt in Lissa's mental voice causing him to smile.

*How did you know?*

*I wasn't sure, I just had a feeling. I thought I would reach out and see.*

*We are connected in more ways than telepathically, dearest. Our hearts are also connected. That must be why you knew.*

*Oh my, Rugal. You are becoming quite the poet. I will have to get my father to write a song from your poet's soul, *laughter**

Rugal laughed as well, out loud, then noticed Johan and Hamideh staring at him, grinning. He smiled weakly in return. "It's Lissa."

"We thought so," Johan winked at his friend. "Please give her our greetings."

Rugal looked off into the distance, his eyes slightly unfocused as he continued his silent conversation. He turned back to his companions, "Lissa returns your greetings and looks forward to seeing you this evening. Lunch will arrive soon." He picked up a stick and using his boot to smooth out the dirt in front of the logs, he gestured for them to sit. "We have some time before lunch arrives. Shall we begin?"

Johan and Hamideh sat quietly, listening to the now-familiar language of the ancient ritual.

"Seidous man *dynamis* ferilux Elayas, Tolan, des Kargolith anthropoi shod."

*We pledge our powers to defend the people of Elayas, Tolan, and Kargolith.*

Normally, they found Rugal's voice comforting, and the peace that accompanied his words would wash over them. But not today. An evil presence who had vowed to destroy them was coming at the end of winter, and they had pledged to defend their people against it. But how could they prepare against the powerful evil forces coming from across the sea?

# CHAPTER
# TWO

"Three kings with three fine steeds, as it should be."
~ Rohan, prince of Kargolith

The sun had begun its downward trek when Rugal finally dropped the stick in the dirt and leaned back, rubbing his arms. He looked down at the marks they had made as they discussed how to spread their forces and let out an exasperated sigh. "We just don't know enough. We don't know exactly when the Neliphim are coming, or where they will make landfall. We don't even know the size of their forces. All we know for certain is that our enemy possesses dark magic. And we don't know its extent, except that the arrow Johan grabbed had the capability to burst into flames." His eyes narrowed. "We need more information. But how do we get it when our enemy lives across the sea?"

Johan stood up and stretched. "I think that is the key," he

murmured. "We need to send someone to gather information for us."

Hamideh nodded. "I think Johan is right. We need to send some spies." He scratched his head. "But who? And how can they cross the Argonean Sea?"

"I don't know," Rugal replied. "But I agree. None of our strategies can work without a better understanding of what we are up against." His stomach growled loudly.

"Has it been that long since lunch?" asked Hamideh, glancing toward the sun and grinning.

"We obviously can't use you for a spy," Johan chuckled, "your stomach would give you away."

Rugal's face reddened, but he managed a smile. "I guess we better go back to the castle. We are expected for dinner, and my stomach is never wrong."

They started down the path and into the forest that separated them from the castle's lawns. None of them noticed the cap hanging from one of the limbs of a tree they passed on their way back to the castle.

"Johan, it is good to see you!" Rohan shouted, jumping off his paint horse. The two brothers hugged.

"I was hoping you would be here!" Johan exclaimed, looking his younger brother up and down. "It seems life in Cargoa suits you."

"It does indeed," Rohan grinned. "Rugal and his family have been most gracious." A mischievous glint came into his eyes. "I have much news to share." He slapped his brother on the back. "And a very special surprise I think you will like." He looked around and spotted Rugal and Hamideh making their way down the path to the castle entrance. "It looks like they've gone on ahead to allow us a little time together. Let's get Jakash some grain, and I'll catch you up."

Rohan looped the reins around his saddle and the twin brothers started walking in the direction of the stables, Rohan's horse following behind. Entering the environs of a well-kept stable was comforting in its familiarity, and Johan took a deep breath and sighed contentedly. Living a nomadic life most of his years, he always appreciated the time he got to spend at the Kargolith's horse training camp, one of the few structures that was a permanent installation. Johan had spent many spring seasons helping with the training of the Kargolith horses, and he always felt rooted when he entered a stable.

Rohan strode over to the grain bins as Jakash made his own way into his stall. The routine of the barn was ingrained in him, and he lifted his head expectantly, awaiting his dinner.

Making soothing noises, Rohan walked over and dumped a measure of grain into Jakash's feed bucket. Johan followed behind with an armful of hay and tossed it in the corner that Rohan indicated. Jakash's water was clean, and Rohan stepped back, a satisfied look on his face. "Yandin is in charge of the stable and has apprentices to care for the horses, but I prefer to take charge of Jakash's care myself."

"It's obvious you have done a fantastic job with him," Johan looked at his brother with pride and affection. "He looks even better than when I last saw you at the Day of Questioning."

Rohan's face lit up at his brother's words. It was hard sometimes to be the brother of the leader of the Kargoliths, but Johan never made him feel less because Rohan was born a minute after him. Both sported the often-found dark, handsome features of the Kargoliths and their Tolan relatives, including thick black hair. Johan had a well-shaped beard, while Rohan chose to remain clean-shaven. Closing the door to Jakash's stall, Rohan pointed to a bench in the barn corridor, and the two slender young men sat down.

"Is it true…" Rohan leaned in eagerly. "Did Rugal give Flash to Hamideh for his coronation?"

Of all the things he might have asked about, it was typical for Rohan to be excited about a horse. Living a nomadic life up until only recently, horses were the lifeblood of the Kargoliths, and Flash was an amazing equine specimen. The big red horse was gifted to Rugal by a local Patriotes during his quest to recover the Ring of Rosin and now that his favorite bay, Tag, was fully recovered from his injury, Flash had not been getting any riding time. Such a fine steed should not go to waste. Johan smiled affectionately at his younger brother. "Yes, it's true. And Hamideh and Flash are a perfect match. They seem to connect the same way Raksh and I do."

"Three kings with three fine steeds," Rohan grinned. "As it should be."

Johan gave his brother a sideways glance. "I wouldn't call myself a king."

"Why not?" Rohan shot back. "The council voted you leader of the Kargoliths. The king of Tolan has approved our territory boundaries and removed their claim. The king of Elayas agreed to those terms. We are now a kingdom, are we not?"

Johan scraped the ground with his foot. He never intended to be a king; all he wanted was what was best for his people. But Rohan was right. The once nomadic Kargoliths who wandered the unsettled territory were no longer. They had gained the right to be called the kingdom of Kargolith, and he supposed a kingdom needed a king. He blew out a noisy breath. "I suppose. It's just very strange to hear myself referred to as a king."

Rohan punched his brother in the shoulder. "You'll get used to it, big brother. You, of all people, would never abuse your position. You don't have to be worried about what people will think. Everyone, Mergolith and Kargolith, is very proud of you."

Johan looked down, reddening slightly. He looked back up and gazed at Rohan. "Alright, but can we change the subject?" he pleaded.

"Sure, King Johan, as you wish," Rohan replied mischievously.

Johan rolled his eyes at his younger brother and cleared his throat. "Didn't you have some news for me? Something about a special surprise?"

Rohan jumped up from the bench and tugged at Johan's sleeve. "Yes! I have been taking classes from the Swordsman. He has a very strategic mind, and I have been learning a lot from him that will benefit our people."

"Like what?" Johan asked, curiosity tinging his voice.

"That's where my special surprise comes in!" Rohan's eyes sparkled, and he could barely contain his excitement. "I have *dynamis!*"

Johan's eyes widened and he leaned back slightly, staring up at his brother, who was obviously enjoying the moment. "What?...How?..."

"The Swordsman was conducting a class in the practice yard." Rohan's face was glowing. "He called me up to help him illustrate a battle move. He swung his sword at me, and I lost my footing, trying to avoid him. I thought for sure he would strike me with the flat of his sword, but something strange happened. He froze for a couple of seconds. Just long enough for me to roll out of his reach."

Johan's eyebrows crinkled as he tried to absorb Rohan's description of what had happened. "So, the Swordsman was about to make contact with his sword, and you were able to stop him?"

"I didn't exactly stop him. I was able to delay him long enough to get out of trouble." He paused, trying to find the right words. "It was as if he froze in place for a brief moment, then continued on the same trajectory after I had reached safety."

Johan rocked back on his heels as he grasped the implications. "That is amazing! Are you able to control it?"

"Not very well," Rohan admitted. He cleared his throat. "Rugal is arranging my entrance into the Sepharim school," he blinked. "With your permission, of course."

Johan gazed at his younger brother for a moment, then stood up and pulled him in for a hug. "I am so proud of you," he mumbled into his ear, pounding his back.

"Are you sure you're not upset?" Rohan stepped back and looked at Johan with concern. "Since, well, you know..."

Johan immediately understood Rohan's apprehension. "No, of course not. If I possess *dynamis*, I am sure it will eventually reveal itself. And if I don't," he shrugged. "I have plenty of other things to worry about." He paused. "When are you thinking of going?"

"Rugal and I have discussed that," Rohan admitted. "We are thinking that I should leave immediately so that by the time the end of winter arrives, I will have a good grasp on what I need to know to use my *dynamis* effectively. It might be useful for...you know..."

Johan's eyes narrowed as he mulled over Rohan's response. He sighed. "It's a shame we must shape our decisions around the threat of the coming invasion, but it makes sense. When will you be leaving?"

"I wanted to get the chance to see you first. In two days with your consent."

What had been a joyous afternoon was now overshadowed by thoughts of the future. "Yes, of course. That makes the most sense." Johan shook his head, trying to banish the solemn mood that thoughts of the coming invasion evoked. He forced a chuckle. "My little brother has *dynamis*. Who would have thought?"

"Certainly not me," Rohan grinned. "But considering *The Fable of the Bird of the Mountains and the Stone of Fire*, perhaps it's not so surprising. After all, Hamideh has *dynamis*, too."

Before Rohan could continue, a blur of feathers flew between the two brothers, circled, and landed on Johan's shoulder, chirping enthusiastically. Johan gave Rohan a questioning look as he tried to soothe the flutebird.

"Lissa usually sends Treble to gather us up for dinner. We best get back," Rohan responded. Treble shook out his feathers and bobbed his head in agreement. Laughing, the two brothers obediently made their way out of the stable and toward the castle.

RUGAL GLANCED around the huge polished wooden table, eyes glowing. It felt wonderful to have friends and family gathered in one place. Mura looked resplendent in her simple pearl-colored gown, Jackal's hand covering hers as they lounged across from him. Rugal's expression softened, and he turned and covered Lissa's hand with his own. Lissa's light brown hair shimmered in the glow of the candles in their sconces, her green gown bringing out the gold specks in her hazel eyes. A fire crackled cheerily in the fireplace. Johan and Rohan sat next to each other, freshly washed faces shining. Rugal was glad that Johan had kept his beard so he could easily tell the two apart.

The group fell to the simple meal with relish. Rugal turned to Tonar, who was sitting on his left, and smiled, "You look rested, my friend."

"I still feel bad that we kidnapped you," Johan interjected, gazing at Tonar. "I know it wasn't easy on you." He put his hand over his heart. "I really admire how you kept the charade that you were Rugal. That was very valiant of you."

Tonar looked down, blushing. "It seemed to be the best course of action at the time." He tugged at his sleeve and then looked back up. "I do feel much better. I have been training with the Swordsman in the mornings and painting in the afternoons." He looked around the table and let out a sigh. "Even if I don't have *dynamis*, it is my hope I can still find ways to contribute."

Rugal punched his closest friend lightly in the shoulder. "Of course you contribute. *Dynamis* or not, you have already sacrificed much for the kingdom."

The Swordsman and Janar nodded their agreement from their seats at the farther end of the table. The Swordsman raised his cup. "To ALL of those who have sworn to defend the people of Elayas, Tolan, and Kargolith, both Sepharim and Patriotes."

Each person raised their cup in return, and the large room reverberated with their cheers. Returning to their meal, the buzz of pleasant conversation continued, providing a brief respite from what lay ahead.

CHAPTER

# THREE

*Sweet memories revive the soul.*
~ Dalbenian Saying

Speckles of light danced through the leaves of the tree as the sun began its morning journey. Finn peered through its branches, watching the Swordsman mount his horse and head towards the tree she had chosen to climb. She balanced on one of its large leafy boughs overhanging the path which meandered through the forest surrounding the castle. From her vantage point, she could see he was alone, and her hands began to tremble with excitement. She took a deep breath to calm her rapidly beating heart.

Dropping into a crouch while maintaining her balance was difficult, but she was able to manage. She brushed a wisp of red hair that had escaped her cap out of her eyes and focused on the man riding toward her. He was riding at a trot, his horse moving exuberantly in the brisk morning air. The Swordsman sat his mount easily, guiding the dappled grey gelding down the path. Finn took another deep breath, and just as the Swordsman came within a few feet of the tree, she jumped down lightly onto the path in front of him.

The Swordsman's horse spooked, leaping to the side at Finn's sudden appearance, but the Swordsman managed to keep his seat. A moment later, he dismounted fluidly from the frightened animal while simultaneously drawing his sword. He crouched a few feet away, muscles tense and ready for combat. Finn, who stood perfectly still, awaited his approach. It seemed her heart would burst out of her chest, it was beating so fast.

The Swordsman looked her up and down and turned pale. "How can this be?" he mumbled to himself.

Finn slowly reached up and pulled off her cap, allowing her long red hair to spill out and onto her shoulders. "Hello, Uncle Zander. I have been waiting a long time to get to meet you."

"How did you get here?" Rugal asked gently. Jackal, Mura, and Lissa had gathered in the library at the Swordsman's behest. They waited patiently as Finn eagerly consumed a plate of food that Mura had ordered brought which had been placed on the table in the center of the room. "I stowed away in the ship that carried the Neliphim's advanced scouting party to your shores," Finn mumbled between bites.

"Let the girl eat," Mura fussed.

Finn looked up gratefully. "It's okay, my Lady. I think if I eat another bite, I shall burst. Living on plants and nuts in the woods does diminish one's appetite."

"You have been living on your own all these weeks?" Rugal jerked back in surprise, eyes wide.

Finn shifted in her chair and looked down, crossing her arms and hugging herself. "It was nothing, Sire. The place I called home is much worse. Here, I could at least be free."

Rugal let out a noisy breath. "Why didn't you come to us sooner?"

Finn looked up and met Rugal's compassionate gaze, and her eyes filled with tears. "I was afraid. I didn't know how I would be received, and I didn't want to go from one slave master to another."

Mura and Lissa came around to Finn's chair and laid their hands on her shoulders. Mura reached down and gently pushed Finn's chin up to look at her. "No one is going to hurt you here. I promise."

Finn nodded hesitantly, wiping her eyes. "Thank you," she whispered.

Mura gazed tenderly at Finn before turning toward the others. "Let's give Finn a chance to rest and regain her composure before she tells her story."

Finn, hand outstretched, shook her head firmly. "No, it's okay. My story must be told for the sake of your kingdoms. We lost several weeks already as I sought the courage to seek out my uncle. We mustn't wait any longer."

Rugal looked at his mother, who nodded. He turned back to Finn and smiled warmly at the young woman who looked to be just a year or two younger than him. "Thank you. That is very brave of you."

Rugal glanced at the Swordsman, who had been sitting quietly the entire time. His shoulders were tense, and his face unreadable as he gazed at his newly found niece. Rugal leaned forward. "How do you know the Swordsman?" he asked gently.

Her voice trembling slightly, Finn looked shyly toward the

Swordsman, and for the first time since they had ushered her into the library, she smiled. "My mother told me about her big brother, Zander. She adored him." She turned toward the others. "His large frame is hard to miss."

"Indeed," Jackal chuckled.

"Mother had told me about his prowess as both a huntsman and horseman. When I saw him from the woods training men in the art of swordplay in the large courtyard every morning, I realized it must be him." She clutched her hands together. "My Uncle Zander." She hesitated for a moment before continuing. "And that he possesses *dynamis*, like my grandfather." She looked back at the Swordsman. "You look just like him."

The Swordsman smiled in return. "It's a miracle you are here, Finn. You look just like your mother." He paused, his eyes hopeful. "How is Zayla?"

Finn looked down, her shoulders drooping as she rubbed her hand against her leg. "She died three years ago... From a fever that ran through our compound." She looked up, tears flowing freely down her cheeks. "She always hoped to be reunited with you someday. You were her hero."

The Swordsman gasped. He lifted his hands up, then let them fall. Tears filled his eyes, and he rubbed his cheek, gesturing Finn to continue.

"I'm sorry to have to tell you about my mother," Finn's voice filled with compassion. "She loved you very much."

Wiping the tears from his eyes, the Swordsman nodded. "She was a wonderful person. I have missed her greatly all of these years." A small smile crept back onto his face as he returned Finn's gaze. "I can see her in your eyes and in the shape of your chin. But you have inherited your grandmother's hair color. I have heard redheads often skip a generation and it seems to be the case here."

"Yes," Finn managed a small laugh. "I have heard about my red hair all my life. It seems your mom was quite a beauty in her day."

"And now?" the Swordsman asked quietly. Everyone at the table held their breath. Hope hung in the air like a tangible blanket enveloping them.

Finn's smile widened. "Well, it's no longer red, but she is still quite beautiful. Grandma and Grandpa live in a hut with my father, in the compound. We have been there all my life. Mother met my father on a work detail. You would like him. He loved my mother very much."

The Swordsman stood up and began to shake. He walked around to Finn, picked her up off of her chair, and hugged her tightly as they both sobbed their joy at being reunited and their sorrow at the loss of Finn's mother and the slavery of their family. Their tears mingled as the others got up and surrounded them, putting their hands on the pair's shoulders and offering comfort through their presence.

Finally, the Swordsman put Finn down and wiped the tears on her cheek with his large thumb. "It is good to meet you, Finn." His face took on a determined expression. "I promise you, we will all be reunited again someday, to live here in Elayas in freedom, or I will die trying." His tone left no doubt as to the sincerity of the big man's words.

Stepping back, the Swordsman's gaze swept the group of people he had come to regard as family. "This is a lot to absorb. I know Finn has much more to share but let us take a break and gather again at lunch."

Jackal stepped forward and squeezed the big man's arm. "Of course. Let's meet in the dining hall at lunchtime. We can resume the conversation then," he said. Noting the nods of agreement all around, everyone moved toward the library doors except for the Swordsman and Finn. The two sat back down, and as Mura was exiting the library, she turned back, looked over her shoulder, and smiled. The Swordsman and Finn were talking animatedly to each other, and her own memory of seeing Rugal after so many years surfaced. She smiled as she watched the two discover joy in finding their family connection.

"Your mother was amazing," the Swordsman leaned back, a smile tugging at his mouth as a childhood memory came to mind. "She was fiercely independent as a child." He shook his head and laughed. "You should have seen her when father told us we had to work the field. She was to throw seeds behind me as I plowed. She was very anxious to meet her friends and was doing her best to hurry me along when our horse decided he was done and would not move, no matter how much I shook the reins."

He gazed at Finn, his eyes sparkling as he replayed the scene in his mind. "She dropped her bag of seed, ran by me, grabbed the plow harness, and climbed aboard that huge horse's back. His name was Dobber. She started yelling and kicking with her skinny legs. It was like watching a flutebird trying to get a dragon moving. The funny thing was, that horse was so flabbergasted at her audacity that he leapt forward and pulled the plow with him.

"My hands were caught in the loops that I had made to hold the reins to the handles, and before I knew it, the plow turned over sideways as it continued to move forward, and I was going along with it." The Swordsman paused and lifted his left thumb to show Finn a faded scar running between the surface of his thumb and forefinger. "My hand got smashed between a rock and the plow handle. The scar has faded but never disappeared."

Finn, her eyes wide as she leaned forward listening with rapt attention, let out a breath. "Then what happened?" she asked.

The Swordsman gazed at the astonishingly familiar face in front of him. "The plow broke and left me in the dirt, but your mother managed to stay on Dobber. I never saw that big draft horse move so fast. She finally got him turned and I clambered up behind her so we could ride home and get my hand doctored." He laughed. "I thought that after that, she wouldn't ride Dobber again, but to my surprise, it was quite the opposite. She and that big goofy horse became inseparable, and he would do anything for her. It was quite a sight seeing a pint-sized girl riding that big draft horse around the village with no saddle or bridle."

Finn closed her eyes and smiled as she pictured her mother as a young girl riding that huge horse. "Mother told me about Dobber, but she never told me that story." She opened her eyes and grinned at the Swordsman. "But she did tell me about the time you two found a couple of bamboo poles and decided to play charge." She pointed just below her right eye. "If you looked really closely, you could still see the circle of the end of the bamboo pole where you accidentally poked her with yours."

The Swordsman laughed at the memory. "Yes, it was not intentional, but father took me behind the woodshed for it." He placed his hand over his heart. "Fortunately, your mother never held it against me."

"No, she didn't," Finn leaned forward and placed her small hand on the Swordsman's huge one. "She was always very proud of you and missed you terribly."

He smiled at his niece. "We have shared sorrow, Finn, but also joy. I am glad you have found me."

Finn sniffled and rubbed her eyes. "I am, too, Uncle Zander."

He gazed at her and shook his head in wonder. "You are so much like your mother." The Swordsman leaned forward in his chair, still smiling. "Come, we best go meet the others in the dining hall. It must be close to lunch time." His expression changed and his eyebrows knit together in concern. "We must understand what we are up against. Perhaps you can help us."

"That is why I came," Finn replied firmly, her eyes flashing with determination.

The Swordsman jerked back and looked carefully at his niece. "Yes, she is just like her mother," he mumbled to himself.

The big man shook himself and stood up. He reached out and awkwardly patted her shoulder. "Come then. Let's go join the others."

CHAPTER
# FOUR

"The apple doesn't fall far from the tree."
~ Leah, The Swordsman's mother

"You said you stowed away on a ship. How did you find us?" Rugal wiped his mouth and put down his napkin. He leaned back in his chair and regarded the slender young woman with open curiosity.

"I was hiding in the woods when the Neliphim spy shot the arrow at you. I saw you enter the river."

Rugal's eyebrows furrowed, and he tilted his head, "Then how did you get to the castle?"

"I walked." Finn smiled. "Elayas is a beautiful country, and the few people I met along the way were helpful in providing direction."

"By yourself?" Rugal stared at Finn with respect. "In an unknown country?"

The Swordsman smiled, his eyes glowing with pride. "Like

our mother would always say, 'The apple doesn't fall far from the tree.' Zayla would be very proud of you."

Finn glanced down, her face flushed, then looked up shyly. "I wanted to find you, Uncle Zander." She glanced around the table, and her voice took on a steely note. "And I want to conquer the Neliphim and bring my people back home."

Rugal leaned forward and gazed intently at Finn. "I want that, too. Your people are our people." He straightened up and looked around the table. "We have all worked together to conquer evil once, and as a result, Elayas has been restored. We are a formidable adversary when we come together with a common goal. We must conquer the evil forces that have held the Swordsman's village hostage across the sea and bring restoration to the families of Elayas that were forced there against their will."

Lissa reached over and placed her hand on Finn's. "We will need your help. Can you describe your journey to our lands?"

"And anything you can tell us about the Neliphim would be helpful. We need to understand what we are up against to formulate an effective strategy," Jackal chimed in.

Finn looked uncertainly at the Swordsman, who pressed his lips together and nodded in return. She squeezed her eyes shut and began to speak in almost a whisper.

"Frakar is the leader of the Neliphim. He took the place of Magdarin, who disappeared many years ago after passing leadership of the Neliphim to Frakar. Magdarin mentored Frakar to be his successor. Frakar has a magical ability to entrap the minds of creatures, bending them to do his will.

"The man you saw on the horse that shot the arrow at King Rugal was Krakos, Frakar's second-in-command. He is a famous warrior among the Neliphim." Finn paused a moment and took a shaky breath, her body visibly tensing. "He is responsible for the raid on Uncle Zander's village so long ago."

She opened her eyes and looked at the Swordsman who was leaning toward her intently, his jaw clenched. "Krakos was one of the men that sought your family's help during the drought." Her eyes filled with tears. "He is the one that led the assault against your village.

"It had been carefully planned. Krakos and his men gained your family's trust and waited until you left on your hunting trip to reduce the number of young men they would have to fight to overcome the village." She drew another shaky breath. "They burned the village to the ground, and the people were stolen to provide the knowledge and labor the Neliphim needed to grow their forests. The Neliphim had watched the villagers tend the forests north of Farath and plant seedlings for wood production. They knew the people of your village had expertise in growing timber, and they needed them to grow wood to build their battle fleet."

Gasps around the table momentarily stopped Finn's narrative as everyone tried to comprehend the horror that the Swordsman and his village had gone through and what their forced labor meant for the coming battle.

Rugal, his eyes wet with compassion, asked, "How could something like this happen in Elayas?"

"You must remember," Jackal replied. "This was during Oldag's reign. King Rosin had been murdered, and our country was in chaos. Marauders, especially in the outer reaches of Elayas, were not uncommon."

Mura nodded in agreement, "It was a terrible time. No one knew what was going on in other places. We were all just trying to survive."

Finn held up her palms. "No one blames Elayas for what happened. We know it was Oldag." She smiled briefly. "We were overjoyed when the news that Oldag had been overthrown was overheard by one of our people in servitude to

Frakar at his castle. That is why I chose to come. Now that the throne of Elayas has been restored to the rightful king, we have hope again." She gazed boldly at Rugal, who returned her gaze and nodded.

*Are you okay? This is a lot to absorb.*

Rugal heard the familiar lilt of Lissa's voice in his head. He appreciated her unique gift of *dynamis* and that she used it judiciously, always having his best interest in mind.

Rugal glanced at his beloved with a brief smile and winked. He turned back to Finn. "Let's start from the beginning. Why are they attacking now? Why not when they captured your village?"

Finn brushed her hair back and met his gaze squarely. "They could not arrive in force and do battle by sea until now. It has taken that long for the trees to mature. You have to wait until the timber is ready for harvest, and that takes years." She frowned. "Years of labor by our people in cultivating the forests, and then the time needed to build the ships. As the trees matured, some of our people were redirected to ship building. An Arlesian master shipbuilder was kidnapped by the Neliphim to supervise. The Neliphim have only recently finished constructing their ships. The battle fleet is now ready."

"How did you get on the ship you arrived on? Can you describe it?"

"The ship is a schooner. It's the first one that has been built to completion since our village was captured so many years ago. The one they had traveled on to get to Elayas was in a state of decay. I have been told it was a miracle that it transported everyone from our village safely to their lands." Finn's eyes grew distant, and she continued. "They can be quite large, with the ability to carry up to 200 men. The one I stowed away on was much smaller. Krakos only took his horse and enough men to crew the ship, and the crew stayed aboard the entire time."

"Then, how did you..."

"Stow away?" Finn gave the Swordsman a shy grin. "You and Grandpa aren't the only ones in the family with *dynamis*."

"And what might yours be?" the Swordsman prodded.

Finn looked down and rubbed her fingers along the table's edge. She took a breath and let it out, then disappeared.

Silence filled the air as everyone gazed in amazement at the place the fiery redhead had occupied.

A few moments passed, and Finn reappeared in a chair that had been unoccupied on the other side of the table.

Everyone cheered, and the Swordsman, his eyes gleaming with pride, walked over to his niece and smiled broadly. "You are just like your mother, full of surprises." He pulled her in for a brief hug and then sat back down.

Finn's shoulders relaxed as the warm acceptance of the people around the table flowed over her.

Jackal leaned forward eagerly. "How long can you remain invisible?"

"Not very long," Finn admitted. "It seems tied to my desire. If I try to disappear for fun, it is only a moment or two." Her shoulders tensed again. "When I was in the hold, if a crew member passed by, I was able to hold it as long as I needed to remain undetected."

Rugal nodded. "That makes sense. Some gifts are tied to need. I first found my *dynamis* when I really wanted to lift a boulder. I was determined not to fail, and that is when I first transformed into a bear."

Finn jerked back and stared at Rugal. "You can turn into a bear?!"

Rugal met her gaze with a grin. "Yes, and any other animal, including birds and insects. Sometimes it's a conscious choice—other times it is an unconscious response to a situation."

Finn nodded. "Yes! That is mine, too."

"You are in good company here," Mura interjected. "We will be able to help you master all of the aspects of your gift."

Lissa nodded, extending her hand toward Finn. "I am still learning about mine." She smiled. "We could learn together."

Tears welled up in Finn's eyes. "I would really like that." She glanced around at the people she had only just met that morning. "I've come home." She wiped her eyes with her napkin and shook herself. "But we have work to do and no time to waste. We must bring everyone home."

Two hours later, Mura stood up and looked pointedly around the table. "Let's give Finn an opportunity to rest. She has been through a lot. We can resume our talk at another time."

Finn started to object, but the Swordsman, gazing fondly at his niece, interrupted. "No, Finn, she is right." He glanced at Lissa. "Could you show Finn to one of the guest rooms so she can get some rest and a warm bath?"

Lissa glanced at Rugal who nodded, and she smiled broadly. "I can do much better than that. There is a bedroom in the family portion of the castle right down from mine." She turned to Finn. "Would you do me the honor of lodging there?"

Finn looked down, smiling shyly. "I would really like that," she whispered.

"Good," Lissa replied. She stood up and linked her arm with Finn's, and the two young women walked out the dining hall doors. Everyone else took their departure as permission to leave until only the Swordsman, Rugal, Jackal, and Mura were left.

"So, what do you think, Swordsman?" Rugal turned to the big man who had become a beloved mentor to him.

The Swordsman leaned back in his chair and blew out a noisy breath. "It's worse than I had imagined." He rubbed his eyes. "The size of their fleet is discouraging. We are going to have to come up with a seafaring strategy in response. Frakar's magical ability to entrap living creatures to do his will poses a huge threat. Not knowing the full potential of Krakos' arrows is disturbing. But we know so much more than we would have otherwise, thanks to Finn."

"Agreed," Rugal shrugged half-heartedly. "But I don't even know where to begin."

"I think it's time to invite Johan and Hamideh to join us," the Swordsman responded, straightening up in his chair. "We must leverage whatever resources are available to save all of our kingdoms."

"What of Arlesia?" Jackal asked. "They also have a stake. The entire continent is at risk."

"Tolan has diplomatic relations with Arlesia," Mura observed. "And Arlesia also borders the Argonean Sea. Perhaps they have a fleet we could build upon."

Treble had been dozing on his customary perch in the dining hall, his head tucked under his wing. Rugal nodded in agreement. He gave a low whistle, and Treble jerked awake. The beautiful blue bird leapt off his perch and winged to land on Rugal's outstretched arm. Rugal smiled affectionately at his feathered friend and took a moment to stroke his feathers. Treble met Rugal's gaze with inquisitive eyes.

"Go find Johan and Hamideh, and lead them back here," Rugal requested.

Treble bobbed his head in understanding. He lifted off

Rugal's arm, winging toward an open window in search of the two young men who had left at dawn on their horses for a brief respite before returning to their kingly duties. Having found out through *The Fable of the Bird of the Mountains and the Stone of Fire* they were related had brought a depth to their friendship that they were eager to explore.

"I remember the day you found Treble on the trail. He was so scruffy and had hurt his wing. You did a great job nursing him back to health," Mura reminisced, watching Treble fly out the window. "How wonderful that a flutebird has befriended you. I think it is amazing that he understands what you say."

"I do, too," Rugal looked down and blushed. "I'm in awe every day, that Treble has chosen to be my companion." He looked back up and held out his hands. "So, what do we know of Arlesia? Should we ask Soldar to join us?"

"Soldar is back in Selba, at the Sepharim school," Mura commented. "He's teaching the history classes." Her eyes lit up. "This first class since Oldag's defeat includes both boys and girls." Jackal gave a low cheer, and the Swordsman grinned. Smiling, Mura continued, "Soldar is spreading his time between the Sepharim school and the schools for those who don't possess *dynamis*."

"As much as I think Soldar would enjoy riding Argothal, I think we can leave him there for now," the Swordsman mused. "I think Hamideh may have a lot of information on Arlesia. During my time at the Tolan Court, emissaries moving between Tolan and Arlesia were very common."

Rugal nodded. "I agree. Much progress is being made in education and that bodes well for the future of Elayas." He settled back in his chair and picked up a piece of bread to nibble. "Let's wait and see what Hamideh has to share."

CHAPTER
# FIVE

"Cast doubt aside so that confidence has room to grow."
~ Felan, Master of the Sepharim

"Arlesia?" Hamideh's eyes widened. "That can be difficult. We have good relations with them, but they tend to keep to themselves. Their emissaries are always cordial, but they don't seem eager to share beyond what is necessary for keeping the peace."

"Well, if they are interested in keeping the peace, joining with us would be in their best interest," the Swordsman responded. He gazed pointedly at Hamideh. "Is Mukatak still part of their diplomatic staff? Surely you remember him?" The big man winked, a mischievous gleam in his eye.

Hamideh swallowed, and red crept up his face. "Please don't tell them about the pony incident," he pleaded.

The Swordsman chuckled. "Do you mean when you had

the pony in the dining hall for Mukatak's visit as a prank? Why would I mention that?"

Hamideh's blush deepened. "Growing up in a castle can be stifling sometimes," he muttered, giving Rugal and Johan a sideways glance.

The hall echoed with laughter as Hamideh fought to regain his composure before continuing. "But to answer your question, yes, Mukatak is still there. He comes every moon."

The Swordsman turned to the others. "The Arlesians have a fleet of ships, something we do not. It is a small fleet primarily used for cargo and fishing, but at least they have one. I think we need to travel to Arlesia and inform them of what is coming and enlist their help. We must all come together if we hope to have a chance against the Neliphim."

Hamideh cleared his throat. "I can go to Arlesia." He paused and gave a wry grin. "Mukatak knows me. I am sure he will be able to get me an audience with King Nakasan. I can explain the coming threat and enlist his help. We don't have time to build a fleet of our own, nor do we have men trained to crew ships. Since Krakos and his troops are coming from the sea, we should have a seafaring force to meet them."

"That sounds like a good plan," Jackal observed. He turned to Rugal. "How about asking Argothal for transport?"

"I think it would be okay for me to return to Tolan by riding Argothal, if he is willing," Hamideh interjected. "But I best take my own horse and ride into Arlesia from there. They are not used to dragons, and no *dynamis* exists among their inhabitants. It may be too overwhelming for them to see a dragon, and that could detract from my mission. Besides," he winked at Rugal. "It would be a fine reason to take Flash for a good day's journey."

"Agreed," Rugal stood up and stretched. "I am so glad you are enjoying his companionship." The big red horse had been hard for Rugal to let go, but he only needed one faithful mount, and Tag was all he could hope for in an equine partner.

Hamideh's eyes lit up. "Flash is everything I could want in a horse. Thank you again for such a magnificent gift."

"I can accompany Hamideh, if that is helpful," Johan interjected.

Rugal smiled at his friend. "Thanks for the offer, but I have something else in mind I was going to request from you."

Johan's eyebrows shot up, and he gazed at Rugal with curiosity. Rugal held up both hands and laughed. "I haven't figured out the details quite yet, but it involves Dungellan. I'll let you know when I do."

Rugal turned back to everyone around the table. "Keep thinking about our options and please let me know anything you think may be helpful. We have a difficult and uncertain road ahead. We will need everyone to participate if we're going to have any hope of success."

Treble chirped his agreement from where he had resumed his perch.

Rugal finished, "I think that's enough for now. Thank you, everyone. Now go get some rest."

As everyone filed out of the room, Rugal was comforted to hear Lissa's voice in his head.

*Have you finished, dearest?*

*For now...*

*Shall we go for a ride then?*

That sounds perfect, Rugal breathed out loud.

*I asked Tonar to saddle Tag for you. We are waiting by the stables.*

Rugal smiled to himself. It was good to feel so loved. Regardless of what the future holds, it was important to remember to take joy in the present moment.

*I'm coming!*

THE FOLLOWING MORNING, everyone gathered in the courtyard. Argothal backwinging onto the flagstones never failed to fill his audience with awe. The natural majesty of the big dragon inspired admiration that transcended culture. Rugal strode forward and wrapped his arms around the fierce creature's lowered head, and Argothal crooned happily in response.

Mura, standing next to Jackal, let out a quick breath. He wrapped an arm around her shoulders and squeezed. "It's still a bit disconcerting," he whispered, smiling gently. "Watching our son hug a dragon."

Mura nodded, her eyes never leaving her son's back, squeezing Jackal's arm in return.

Rugal stepped away and faced his draconic friend. "Thank you for responding to my request," he addressed the dragon formally. Before he could continue, Treble winged past him, chirping, to land on Argothal's head. He puffed out his blue-feathered chest and looked at Rugal expectantly.

"And thank you, Treble, for finding Argothal." Rugal smiled affectionately at his avian friend.

"Why didn't you ask Lissa to summon him?" Johan asked, eyebrows raised.

"It seems there is some limitation on Lissa's ability to communicate with Argothal. He must be in her vicinity." Rugal grinned broadly and winked at Lissa. "Fortunately, we have no such limitation."

Argothal craned his neck toward Lissa, *I'm sorry I couldn't hear you.*

Rugal could hear Lissa's gently chiming laughter in his head.

*It's not your fault, Argothal. It's the nature of my dynamis. I am still grateful for our connection!*

The dragon's right eye focused on Lissa, the iris soft with gold specks glittering throughout. *As am I.*

Argothal straightened back up and gave a gentle shake, causing Treble to squawk as he fought to keep his balance and his audience to move away a bit. He slung his head around toward Rugal, who had not moved.

"Could you please transport Hamideh back to Tolan?" Rugal asked.

The dragon dipped his head in agreement, and Rugal continued. "I may have another request after you have brought Hamideh to his castle. We have much to do to prepare for the coming battle. Would you mind returning here afterward?"

The huge dragon nodded his head a second time, his blue and green scales shining in the morning sun. Rugal stepped forward and scratched the scales on his face affectionately.

Argothal gazed at Rugal and croaked several times. Rugal smiled. He didn't need Lissa to interpret for him. "Thank you, Argothal. You are a good friend."

Rugal stepped back as Hamideh eagerly approached Argothal. Smiling broadly, he greeted Argothal and, grabbing his scales, clambered up the foreleg the dragon offered. Settling himself on Argothal's back, he looked down at Rugal, his face shining with excitement. Yandin, the young royal blacksmith, ran up to Argothal, his hand clutching an envelope. He looked up at Hamideh shyly and held the envelope up toward him.

"Greetings, Sire," Yandin breathed out in a gasp. "Could you please pass this to Princess Gillian upon your return?"

Hamideh's eyebrows shot up, and he gazed intently at the young man. He glanced at Rugal who was trying unsuccessfully to hide a smile. "How do you know my sister?"

Yandin's cheeks reddened. "I don't, Sire. But Lady Lissa has told me about her. She suggested I write her a note of introduction." He held his breath and continued to hold the envelope in the air toward Hamideh.

Lissa quickly ducked behind Mura, then peeked around her and met Hamideh's gaze with a grin on her face, her eyes gleaming mischievously. Finally, Hamideh blew out a long breath, his expression remaining serious.

He slowly extended his hand, took the envelope, and stuffed it into his shirt. "I will pass it on," he replied, voice stern.

Yandin let out the breath he had been holding and gazed up at Hamideh. "Thank you, Sire!" Before Hamideh could comment further, the young blacksmith ducked away and ran up the path to the stables.

Rugal chuckled and slapped his friend's leg, then his expression turned serious. "I have asked Treble to accompany you so that you can send a message through him after you meet with Mukatak. You can write a note and affix it to Treble's leg. We will be able to communicate much faster that way."

Treble interjected with an energetic chirp, bobbing his head in agreement. He hopped to a dip between two of Argothal's scales, settling himself in for the ride.

"That sounds like an excellent plan," Hamideh responded. "As soon as I have news of the results of our meeting, I will send you a report."

He leaned down and clasped Rugal's arm. Johan stepped forward, grinning up at his friend and the two also clasped arms.

After observing the three young leaders of their kingdoms, the Swordsman and Jackal's eyes met. The two men held a long glance filled with emotion. "We've come a long way since

Cargoa and stealing the Key of Power," the Swordsman whispered.

"Yes," Jackal shook his head in memory. His eyes narrowed, and he turned his gaze back toward the young men. "But we still have a long way to go." He looked back at the Swordsman and changed their dynamic with a single word. "What think you, *Tamadar*. Are they up to it?"

The Swordsman pondered Jackal's question carefully. As leader of the Sepharim, he had much to consider. He finally let out a breath. "They have each proven themselves in various ways these past months. If they aren't, I don't think any of us are."

Uncertainty hung like a blanket, covering them. Shaking it off, the two men forcibly resumed a more hopeful demeanor. No need to cause unnecessary alarm by expressing their fears. The task ahead was already challenging enough without casting doubt on the abilities of these young leaders.

# SIX

"It's like flying!"
~ Finn, riding a horse for the first time

The sun had just begun its skyward journey. Johan's younger brother Rohan sat astride his paint horse, eager to start his next adventure as a student at the Sepharim school but reluctant to leave his new friends. He smiled shyly and waved to everyone from the castle who had gathered to see him off. Then, he turned his horse in the direction that would take him to Selba.

Watching Rohan disappear through the trees, Finn turned and looked up at the Swordsman with a shy smile. "Uncle Zander," she began hesitantly. "I have always wanted to ride a horse, like my mom. We were never allowed to do such things under the bondage of the Neliphim."

The Swordsman smiled back. "Then ride we shall. I have some time now, if you like."

Finn gasped. "It's so different here." She bounced up and down, her eyes shining. "I would like that very much!"

The Swordsman sought out Yandin, who had been part of the crowd watching Rohan leave. He found the young man that Rugal had chosen to be the royal blacksmith chatting with Tonar in the stable yard. "Yandin, Tonar, good to see you both," the Swordsman addressed them. "Yandin, can you recommend a mount for Finn? We are going for a ride."

"Certainly, sir," Yandin nodded. He turned to Tonar. "Would you mind getting the Swordsman's dappled grey gelding? I'll go get Lady Mura's white mare. I am sure the lady will be glad for Misteria to get some exercise, and she has good instincts for taking care of her rider."

THE TWO STARTED OFF SLOWLY, but the path was inviting and the weather brisk—soon they found themselves at a gallop, Finn easily sitting her mare, until laughing, they pulled the horses up under a tree in a nearby meadow.

Finn giggled, her eyes big. "No wonder mother loved riding Dobber. It's like flying!"

The Swordsman gazed at his newly-found niece with pride. "You are a natural, Finn. Just like her."

"Thanks! This is one of the best days of my life." Misteria craned her neck around and nuzzled Finn's foot as if in agreement.

She reined the mare around to face the Swordsman. Her eyebrows knit together, and the expression on her face changed to determination. "We must bring everyone back home."

The Swordsman's horse jigged, and the Swordsman patted

his neck. "We will do our best, Finn. What else can you tell me about the Neliphim lands and people? That would be most helpful."

Finn looked into the distance for a moment, then met the Swordsman's gaze. "I think we have to go there. I can't provide the details you need." She hung her head, and Misteria nickered softly. "We were forced to stay in the compound. We only were allowed to leave it to work and when we were in the forests cultivating the timber, we were supervised by the Neliphim."

"It's okay, Finn. The important thing is that you managed to get here." He paused and scratched his head, thinking. He finally looked back at Finn. "I think we need to follow Krakos' example and send a spy mission to their lands. It seems to me we will have to do battle on several fronts." A perplexed look crossed his face. "This is beyond my experience. As leader of the Sepharim I have encountered many things, but never a threat from seafarers. Combined with what you shared about Frakar's ability to entrap a living creature to do his bidding and not knowing the full potential of Krakos' arrows present formidable obstacles." He rubbed his chin, thinking out loud. "I can ask Argothal for transport. I can fly undetected at night. Dragons have good night vision, so it shouldn't be too difficult." He looked at Finn and raised his eyebrows. "Do you know how far it is across the sea?"

"I wish I did, Uncle. I don't know the distance but perhaps we can calculate it from how many days we were at sea." She pursed her lips in thought, straightening in the saddle. "We were at sea six days, but we anchored at night. On the third day, we anchored on an island. I heard one of the crew members say we were traveling northeast at around eight knots, and I would say we traveled around sixteen hours a day."

"Hmmm," the Swordsman's expression grew thoughtful. "A horse travels at the same pace." He rubbed his cheek. "But ten hours is more realistic for horses. So, if we were traveling by horseback, it would take us ten days." He paused, biting his lip and gazing into the distance. "But you said an island is halfway between?"

"Yes," Finn nodded. "I didn't leave the ship, but the others did. It had some trees and a freshwater lake further inland that I could see from the ship."

The Swordsman nodded to himself and then asked, "Is it big enough for a dragon to land?"

"Easily, I would say," Finn replied. She stared at the Swordsman. "Why?" The Swordsman didn't answer immediately, and comprehension dawned on her face. "I'll go with you!"

Finn stood up in her stirrups in her excitement. "I can show you the compound where your parents and my father live and Frakar's castle." Finn's eyebrows shot up, and she bounced in her stirrups, causing Misteria to move forward. She settled back into her saddle, and the mare came to a stop. "We can bring the battle to Frakar and rescue our village instead of waiting for him to come to Elayas!"

The Swordsman held up a hand in a calming gesture. "One step at a time, youngster," he said in a soothing voice, although his mind was racing with the possibilities. He glanced back over at his niece. Finn's fiery red hair was windblown, cascading around her face and shoulders. She sat easily on the white mare, obviously already at home in the saddle. A sweet memory of her mother riding Dobber around their village came to the Swordsman's mind, and he couldn't help but smile.

The air was brisk and inviting. Just as he was about to suggest they resume their ride, his horse jigged again. This time, the Swordsman could tell it was because the big horse sensed something, and his body tensed. He turned his large frame from side to side in the saddle, craning his head around to catch a glimpse of what was disturbing his trusted gelding, when Tonar, racing his black mare, burst out of the woods behind them.

Tonar reined up beside them, his face crinkled with urgency. "You must come back to the castle!"

"What happened?" The Swordsman pulled his horse around to face the young man who had become a trusted friend to Rugal, having earned a place in his inner circle when he protected Rugal's identity at great personal risk.

"Ethiod's here...and he has news."

Finn looked at the Swordsman, tilting her head to one side in silent question.

"Ethiod is Lissa's father," he explained. "He is, among other things, a master of the Sepharim." He nodded to Tonar, and they urged their horses into a gallop back to the castle.

"ETHIOD, it is good to see you!" the Swordsman strode into the library, with Tonar and Finn close behind. He wrapped an arm around Finn and pulled her forward. "I want you to meet my niece, Finn."

Finn looked into Ethiod's serene blue eyes and smiled shyly.

Ethiod returned her gaze with a gentle smile. "Welcome, Finn. It is good to meet you." He held out his hand. "My daughter Lissa has told me a little bit about your extraordinary adventures." He winked. "I can see how you are kin to the Swordsman." His expression turned serious. He swept his hand across his silvery hair and gestured to the table. "Come, everyone. Please sit down. I have important news to share."

Rugal glanced around the table to make sure everyone had arrived. Mura and Jackal sat in their usual places side by side. Johan was on his left, and Lissa his right. Tonar slid into a seat across from Finn. Ethiod took a seat across from Rugal. "Sire, if I may?"

Rugal had grown accustomed to the formality of court and instinctively inclined his head, granting permission. Jackal squeezed Mura's hand under the table, and they shared a brief smile.

Ethiod cleared his throat. "As most of you know, Soldar and I have been in Selba. Rugal," he gave the young king a quick smile, "has appointed us in charge of revitalizing education in Elayas. Soldar has taken charge of establishing schools for those who do not possess *dynamis*, and I am charged with creating additional schools for the Sepharim. Soldar is also serving as an instructor of history where needed." He paused, rubbing his hand tiredly across his eyes. "I bring disturbing news. Soldar has been kidnapped."

Mura's hand flew to her chest, and she stood up with a gasp. "How? Who? Why?"

"How does Mura know Soldar?" Finn whispered to the Swordsman.

"He was a member of her cousin King Rosin's court before Oldag came to power. Soldar is a scholar with a broad knowledge of Elayas and our history," he whispered back.

Finn nodded, and both turned their full attention to Ethiod's next words.

"I'm sorry, Mura," Ethiod's voice filled with compassion. "He was out for his evening stroll along the banks of the Selba River when a man emerged from some trees near the bank. A Patriotes was nearby and observed what happened. The man drew an arrow from his quiver," Ethiod paused and held up his hand at the look of horror on Mura's face. "Soldar was not harmed. The man shot the arrow at Soldar, and something happened that the Patriotes could not find an explanation for. When the arrow came within a few feet of Soldar, it exploded into a cargo net, and instead of striking him, it enveloped him." Ethiod shook his head. "It had to be magic."

"What happened next?" Mura choked out.

"That is where the details are rather fuzzy. According to the Patriotes, the man with the bow and arrows leapt up the bank, tied a rope to the handles of the cargo net, and cast the rope into the river. He stood next to Soldar on the bank and pulled out what looked to be a slender wooden whistle. He blew the whistle, and a huge creature erupted from the waters. According to the Patriotes, it looked like a dragon, except it was a sea creature. It had a huge, scaled snake-like body, with a triangular head that had fins fanning out the sides and fierce teeth protruding from its mouth. Its eyes had a strange cast to them, glowing yellow."

Ethiod paused for breath, allowing his audience a moment to process what he was saying. "The creature took the rope in its mouth and lifted Soldar off the bank. It carried him in the cargo net."

"What about the archer?" the Swordsman asked.

Ethiod shook his head. "It seems beyond belief. The sea creature lowered its head and affixed to its neck was a saddle. The archer leapt onto its neck and climbed into the saddle. The creature raised his head so that it towered above the river. The archer cut the ropes of the cargo net, grabbing Soldar by the arms, and Soldar had no choice but to clamber onto the saddle behind him. The Patriotes said that the sea creature turned and began to speed through the water at an incredible rate, westward."

"They must have been heading to the Great River. It flows all the way to the Argonean Sea," Jackal interjected.

Ethiod nodded in agreement, "The archer must have snuck into the Great River on the back of the sea creature, riding it to the Selba River to kidnap Soldar. They could then reverse course, and head back out to sea." He frowned, and his brow crinkled with concern. "The sea creature must have magical abilities to be able to move so fast."

"It must be the same man that shot the arrow at me. The arrow that burst into flames. And we don't know the full potential of his magic arrows." Rugal blew out a breath of frustration. "But why?" he asked, wincing at the thought of Soldar captured by the man the Ring of Rosin had called evil.

"Soldar is a logical choice. He knows Elayas better than anyone, and he is familiar with our court. He can provide invaluable information to the marauders for their invasion." The Swordsman turned to Finn. "Do you think that was Krakos?"

"I am almost sure of it," Finn nodded, her eyes flashing. "He possesses the magical arrows. I know of no other. Frakar has given Krakos the whistle to control the leviathan."

"Leviathan?" Rugal turned to Finn. "Do you mean the sea creature the Patriotes described? I have not seen one before."

"Yes," Finn responded. "Leviathans possess the magical ability to move supernaturally fast. Krakos often uses one for transportation. It is well-known among the Neliphim that Frakar is able to control creatures—he entraps their minds with his *dynamis*. He controls the leviathan and forces it to obey Krakos. The leviathan must respond to the whistle."

"What of Soldar?" Mura interrupted. "Do you think they will hurt him?"

"Not while they find him useful," Finn replied. "They are barbaric, but they aren't stupid. He is more useful to them alive, otherwise they wouldn't have gone to all of this trouble to capture him."

The Swordsman stood up, and all eyes turned to him. The change was evident in his demeanor; he was now assuming the mantle of Tamadar, leader of the Sepharim. "Thank you for bringing us this information, Ethiod," he nodded at the Sepharim master. He looked at Mura with a compassionate gaze, then turned to face everyone at the table. "Obviously, we must rescue Soldar. We also need to mount an expedition to spy on the enemy and get as much information as possible." He glanced at Finn, who sat holding her breath. "I propose to go, with Finn as my guide, to their lands."

CHAPTER

# SEVEN

"You can't do everything yourself. You also must trust the
people around you."
~ Lissa, future queen of Elayas

After the initial noise of everyone voicing their objections of putting the Swordsman and Finn at risk died down, Jackal leaned forward. "How would you go?"

The Swordsman looked at Rugal and grinned. "Never pass up the opportunity to ride a dragon."

"But wouldn't it be too far for Argothal to fly?" Rugal asked.

"I thought that might be the case, too," the Swordsman replied, "but Finn was able to clarify the distance involved and the existence of an island halfway between our continent and the Neliphim lands." He met Rugal's gaze. "It is doable."

"I think I should go," Rugal replied, his eyes flashing. "As

commander-in-chief of Elayas in wartime, I need to understand our enemy."

The Swordsman held up a hand, stopping Mura and Lissa
from speaking. "Sire, I agree you must have that information,
but you must also not put yourself at unnecessary risk when
Elayas is in need of you. You have much to coordinate here to
prepare for what lies ahead." He looked at Rugal sympathetically. "I know you want to take action, but sometimes the
wisest thing a leader can do is delegate."

Rugal glanced at Ethiod, who nodded his agreement.

"The Swordsman is correct," Ethiod said. "He and Finn are
the right ones for the job." He then turned to Mura. "What
about Legas? He may be a good addition as well."

"Legas?" Tonar exclaimed. "The same Legas that met us in
Laran when we were pursuing the Ring of Rosin?"

"Yes, indeed," Ethiod replied, eyes twinkling. "Legas is a
Sepharim master and a man of many talents, including cartog-
raphy. He would be invaluable in spying out the lands of the
Neliphim. He is also very good at thinking on his feet."

All heads turned toward Rugal, who let out a disappointed
sigh and shrugged his shoulders. "I agree. The Swordsman,
Finn, and Legas make the most sense." His gaze fell on the
Swordsman, and he lapsed into formal court etiquette.
"Tamadar, when will you be leaving?"

The Swordsman glanced at his niece, who nodded her
readiness. "As soon as Argothal can transport us. We can pick
up Legas on our way." The big man rubbed his chin. "We have
two full days of flight with an opportunity to rest in-between
on the island. We want to arrive in the enemy territory at night
so we can remain undetected. Hmmm..." He paused, his eyes
narrowed in thought. "We will want to leave in the morning
hours when it is time. We'll be able to spend the night on the
island, travel the following day, and arrive at nightfall." He

turned to Finn. "Will we be able to easily hide once we get there?"

Finn bounced up and down, trying to reign in her excitement. "Yes, Uncle. None of the Neliphim ever enter the compound, and we have a secret way into and out of it." She looked down, her shoulders drooping. "They know we have no alternative other than to live there if we are to survive." She shook herself and looked back up, straightening with a determined set to her chin. "Our people will be eager to help. They can hide us while we spy out the land."

The Swordsman smiled at his niece and turned back to Rugal. "We now have a plan, with your approval, of course."

Rugal rubbed his nose, glancing around the table and noting each person looking toward him expectantly.

*Ethiod's right, you know. You can't do everything yourself. You also must trust the people around you. They are your inner circle for good reason. They have each earned their place.* Lissa's voice in his head was both comforting and frustrating, especially when he knew she was right.

*I know, dearest. I just hate putting others in danger.*

*I understand. But we are all in danger until we defeat the coming menace,* Lissa continued reasonably in the voice he had come to treasure.

Rugal stood up and met the Swordsman's eyes. "Well thought-out, Tamadar. Proceed," he paused, and his expression became firmer, "with care. I would hate to miss out on the meal you still owe me."

"Of course, Sire," the Swordsman ducked his head. "At the best tavern in Cargoa."

"You still haven't gone?" Jackal interrupted them, chuckling. "I thought you promised to take Rugal after he retrieved the Key of Power from Oldag's possession."

The Swordsman uncharacteristically blushed. "I've been a bit busy these past weeks," he mumbled.

"Understandable," Rugal added dryly. "I have had a few adventures myself since then."

Waiting for the laughter to subside from both the Swordsman's discomfiture and Rugal's understatement, Ethiod addressed the group. "I want to emphasize it is critical that we rescue Soldar. He has knowledge no other of our generation possesses."

The mood changed at Ethiod's pronouncement, as the gravity of Soldar's kidnapping was felt by all. Not only was he a beloved friend in need of rescue, but he may also hold the key to who would prevail in the coming battle.

Ethiod turned to Finn and smiled gently. "We have need of your knowledge, young one. Please share with us the possibilities regarding Soldar's whereabouts." He glanced at the Swordsman, who was leaning forward attentively. "Perhaps we can formulate a plan for his rescue."

Finn nodded, her eyebrows crinkled and expression serious. "I am fairly certain of where he would have been taken," she bit her lip. "He will be in Frakar's castle. I think I may know of a way to get to him."

"Very good," the Swordsman stood up. "I need to send word to Legas. We can work out the details on our way." He turned to Rugal. "I think it best to lay some preliminary plans before I leave."

Rugal stood up. "I agree, I have some ideas I would like to discuss." He walked over to one of the storage cabinets that were sprinkled strategically throughout the library and pulled out a map. He brought it back to the table and unrolled it, spreading it out onto the polished wooden surface. "We have many great resources to defend our kingdoms. I have been thinking about how we can coordinate our efforts." He brushed the hair out of his eyes.

"When we came together to battle Oldag, we were in a much smaller area geographically. We also had a plan in place, and Patriotes in every city to coordinate that plan. The actual battle time and place were known, and we understood our adversary." He looked up, his forehead creased with concern. "This time, we know nothing about our enemy. We don't know his strengths or weaknesses, or even where and when he will appear."

Moving over to his son's side, Jackal pointed at the kingdom of Kargolith on the map. "Each kingdom has strengths we can leverage. Kargoliths are known for their exceptional horsemanship."

Johan straightened up in his chair, smiling. "We are ready and at your disposal."

Nodding appreciatively, Jackal pointed next to the kingdom of Tolan. He turned to Mura, eyebrows raised.

Mura walked over to the map and stared down at it for a few moments. She looked up and smiled. "My cousin had a very strong relationship with King Handerbin. The Tolan's royal militia has an extraordinary cadre of archers. We even sent some of our people to be trained in archery by them. I daresay Hamideh is continuing that tradition."

The Swordsman grinned. "Our castle guardsmen have been training diligently in swordsmanship. I believe Elayas can supply a most effective legion of swordsmen."

"I had an idea about that." Rugal glanced at Johan. "I met an extraordinary warrior skilled in swordplay during my journey to recover the Ring of Rosin. He is a Kargolith, and his name is Dungellan. I would like to propose he meets with the Swordsman, and if the Swordsman finds his skills satisfactory and Dungellan is agreeable, that Dungellan serves as leader of our legion of swordsmen."

Johan jerked back in surprise, processing Rugal's words. It was unprecedented for such an invitation to be extended; someone leading the castle guardsmen of another's kingdom was unheard of. The trust Rugal was extending was almost overwhelming. He looked at the Swordsman, who nodded his assent.

"I will talk to Dungellan. I think he will be honored," Johan managed to reply.

Rugal grinned. "Argothal can transport you. He is returning here after bringing Hamideh to Tolan." He paused for a moment, mentally calculating the distance and flight time. "He should be back this afternoon. After he has had an opportunity to rest and eat, I will ask Argothal to take you home and return with Dungellan. That will give the Swordsman a chance to meet and get to know Dungellan before Argothal transports the Swordsman to the lands of the Neliphim. If all goes well, Dungellan will remain here in the Swordsman's place while he is on the spy mission with Finn and Legas."

Johan nodded his agreement, eyes glowing at the prospect of another dragon ride, and the honor being bestowed upon his countryman.

Ethiod had remained quiet after his initial pronouncement of Soldar's kidnapping and request for help in his rescue. He cleared his throat, drawing everyone's attention. "The Sepharim must be ready to mobilize. I have been working with Janar and the Swordsman." He smiled at Jackal, who looked askance at the Swordsman before leaning forward, his eyes riveted on Ethiod. The tall Sepharim master's normally serene blue eyes took on a steely edge. "We also have been thinking of the coming battle and will be prepared."

The Swordsman coughed and met Jackal's gaze. "I know

you wanted to be in the midst of the battle, but we need you at the castle to help Rugal coordinate our troops. You are our best strategist. The Sepharim will be led by Ethiod and Janar."

Jackal opened his mouth to protest, then shut it and nodded.

"But what of the Patriotes?" Tonar looked earnestly around the table. "We have an entire network in place across Elayas, with counterparts in Tolan and Kargolith. Many of us with no *dynamis* have a strong desire to defend our homes."

Rugal smiled broadly. "That is where you come in, Tonar. I am placing you in charge of the Patriotes network."

Tonar's jaw dropped. "But I'm not qualified. I have never..."

"Oh, you are more than qualified," Jackal interrupted. "You have shown your loyalty ten-fold, and you are quick-witted. You are perfect for the job."

Tonar glowed at Jackal's words and blushed as everyone nodded their agreement.

"What about me?" Lissa asked almost plaintively.

"Why, that's easy," Rugal gazed fondly at his future bride. "You and Mura will have a critical role in directing communications between our various factions. You will be able to communicate directly with me, of course, but even more importantly, we are reactivating our signal corps."

Tonar's eyebrows raised, and he tilted his head at Rugal. "Signal corps? What's that?"

"Fire beacons maintained and monitored in order to signal when an invading force is sighted." Rugal's face broke out into a grin. "Something I learned about from Soldar, when he was tutoring me in the history of Elayas. At the time, I did not appreciate the gift of knowledge Soldar was giving me. We have learned so much from him."

"We must get him back!" Mura interjected. "He has sacrificed much for Elayas."

"We will," the Swordsman replied. "I won't stop until Soldar and my village have come home."

No one in the room doubted the sincerity of the big man's words. Finn gazed at her uncle and muttered inaudibly under her breath the sentiment felt by everyone. *If only he can.*

# CHAPTER
# EIGHT

"It's easier for a friend to turn into an enemy, than an enemy to
turn into a friend."
~ Raza, philosopher of Tolan

Soldar rubbed his shoulders and back, trying to ease the pain. He didn't know if it came from his brief time in the cargo net, or the fast-paced journey on the back of the sea creature as the beast cut through the ocean waves at an alarming rate. Either way, it was an unpleasant reminder of his present predicament. He pushed his glasses firmly onto his nose, grateful he had not lost them during the events that brought him here. By his estimation, it was a half-day's journey, at a speed that could only be achieved magically. Now, if he only knew where "here" was. He looked down at his clothing. Typically rumpled, they had finally dried.

Arriving in the dark of night, he was grateful he had been escorted to a room that was obviously used for living quarters with a fireplace rather than the dungeon he had imagined while riding the giant sea creature. His transport must have been a leviathan, the sea creature of ancient lore.

His natural curiosity that had served him so well during his academic career surfaced, and he got up off the couch he had collapsed on four hours earlier. Looking about the well-furnished room, he noticed a window in one corner. Stretching the kinks out of his shoulders, he walked over to investigate what might be on the other side. Opening the shutters, he looked out at the coming dawn, the sun's light streaking across what must be the castle grounds. Rows of trees rolled off into the distance, and a few people were meandering about. Before he could ponder any further, there was a sharp rap on the door. He could hear the bar used to lock it from the other side disengage, and the door opened.

Soldar strode to the door and carefully peered at the young boy waiting on the other side.

The young boy bowed. "You are wanted in the main hall, sir. I have been sent to accompany you."

"Who are you?"

"I am one of the servants of Frakar's household."

"So strange," Soldar looked down, mumbling to himself. He looked back at the boy. "Why am I here?"

The boy's eyes widened. "You don't know?" he stuttered.

"No idea," Soldar admitted.

"But you are the redeemer," the boy blurted out. "Frakar says so."

"The who?" Soldar brushed his sparse brown hair out of his eyes, perplexed,

"The wise one. The one that holds the knowledge of the Key of Power."

"I don't know who Frakar is or what you are talking about." He sighed. "There must be some mistake."

The boy shook his head forcefully. "There can't be. Frakar never makes any mistakes."

SOLDAR'S HEAD swiveled back and forth as they walked through the castle to the entrance of the main hall. The elaborate rugs depicting battles and hunting scenes hanging on the walls were somehow vaguely familiar, like one would find in Elayas, something he wasn't expecting after traversing an ocean to another land. How that happened in the space of hours rather than days could only be magic. Unlike Argothal, the leviathan was not friendly, and it had been very focused on its task of transporting its riders without any other type of interaction. Its long flexible body had an interesting symmetry, its bluish-grey scales resembling a dragon but with a triangular head that had fins protruding from its cheeks and wings that seldom rose above the waves. He wasn't sure if the beast could fly or if the wings were only used to help propel it through the water. When Soldar attempted to thank the creature for bringing them to their destination safely, it ignored him and swam away as quickly as possible.

The doors to the main hall were open, and they entered the huge chamber. The young boy pointed across the room to a figure sitting on a throne. "You may approach him when he signals you with his hand," he whispered. Bowing once again, he turned on his heel and made his way out of the room, leaving Soldar alone with the person who must have ordered his kidnapping and was presumably the king of the land he had been brought to.

The hall was warm, but Soldar felt a chill go down his spine. He stared across the room at the figure in the chair, waiting for the person on the throne to signal him to approach. As an expert on court etiquette, Soldar typically had tremendous patience and respect for royalty, but having been dragged through an ocean against his will shortened his capacity for patience. He blew out a noisy breath, shoved his glasses back into place again, brushed his hair back, and strode forward, his jaw and his fists uncharacteristically clenched.

Approaching within a few feet of the throne, Soldar's eyes widened in recognition, and opening his hands, he let out a gasp. "Ferrous?"

The man sitting on the throne stood up, and their eyes locked.

"Soldar." A long pause. "It's been a long time."

Soldar hesitated, his eyes darting from the man in front of him to the walls on either side. More tapestries hung from the walls, and he realized why they looked so familiar. They were the same tapestries that had gone missing from the castle in Cargoa so many years ago, around the same time of Ferrous' disappearance. They were woven by Meron, Ferrous' father, who was a master weaver commissioned to do the royal tapestries for the castle. As a newly appointed scholar to King Rosin's court, Soldar remembered the scandal well. Their whereabouts were never located.

His eyebrows crinkled in confusion, and he had to steady himself. He turned his gaze back to Ferrous. "I don't understand," he shook his head. "You went missing twenty-five years ago. Before Oldag overthrew King Rosin."

Ferrous smiled, but it did not reach his eyes. He straightened his shoulders, pulling the red robe he wore casually about them into place. His narrow face and sharp chin were an extreme contrast to Soldar's pudgy countenance.

"And you didn't come find me..."

His words hung in the air between the two old friends.

Soldar gaped at Ferrous and finally shook his head. "I don't understand. We tried."

Ferrous slammed a fist into his side, and his gaze became piercing. "Not hard enough."

Soldar shook his head. "Not true. We searched for a long time. But when Oldag began his rebellion, everything else had to be shoved aside. We were fighting for our lives, and Rosin lost his. By then, we were just trying to survive."

Ferrous bared his teeth. "Not my problem. You abandoned me."

Seeing that it didn't matter what Soldar said in his defense, he decided to try a different tact.

"How did you steal the tapestries from the castle, and why bring them here?"

Ferrous's eyes softened. "I wanted them. They were all that was left of my family after my father died. The one who kidnapped me was a man of great power. He was able to transport them through his magic. They are a reminder of where I came from." He paused, his expression growing stormy, "and my betrayal."

Soldar rocked back on his heels, holding a hand to his throat in dismay. "This man of great power. Is he the evil one of the oracle? The one the Ring of Rosin spoke of?"

"No," Ferrous shook his head. "He was called Magdarin, and he is no longer with us. Krakos is the one that possesses magic through his arrows and will lead the invasion." His eyes drilled into Soldar's. "I am called Frakar, the name given to me by Magdarin. He was my mentor." He paused, eyes gleaming. "Magdarin named me to take his place. I am the leader of the Neliphim, even though I am not of them."

Soldar stared in disbelief. "What happened to you?" he whispered. "We played together in the schoolyard at Selba. You graduated from the Sepharim school with honors. Your *dynamis* is one of the most powerful in the history of our king-dom. Why have you turned against us?"

"I was kidnapped by Magdarin because of my *dynamis*. His spies had informed him of my ability to entrap the mind of creatures and he wanted to use it to capture the leviathan you rode here on. Once I arrived, I fought against him, waiting to be rescued. After many months, I lost hope. Magdarin offered me an apprenticeship. He said if I agreed to join him, I would become his second-in-command, leading the Neliphim. He offered me riches and my own lands." He lowered his gaze briefly. "I was devastated when no one arrived to rescue me. Magdarin was kind to me. I agreed."

Soldar reached out a hand toward his old friend. "I am sorry, Ferrous. It was not our intent to abandon you. You must believe that."

Ferrous regarded his old playmate with a painful expres-sion. "I don't. And I intend to make Elayas pay." He cocked an eyebrow. "You can join me, Soldar. With your knowledge of the Key of Power and my *dynamis*, we can rule the entire world."

"That's why you kidnapped me," the pudgy man sputtered. "To destroy Elayas?"

Ferrous's demeanor softened, and he sighed. "Ironic, isn't it. My best friend holds the knowledge that will determine who wins the coming battle. You betrayed me once. I am hoping you don't choose to betray me a second time."

Soldar's eyebrows shot up. "Best friend? What friend treats another this way? Kidnapping me and asking me to betray my kingdom?" He took a breath and strode forward, closing the gap between him and Ferrous, his eyes blazing. "I will never do anything against the best interests of Elayas. The secret of the key will not be yours!"

"So, you admit you know it," Ferrous leaned in and grabbed Soldar by the shoulders.

Soldar looked up at his oldest friend, his eyes moist. "I will die before revealing it to you."

"Your choice," Ferrous replied, thrusting Soldar violently away. He stepped back and called out, "Guard, come return the prisoner to his room."

A tall, well-muscled man with a sword emerged from an entrance off to one side. He approached Soldar. "Come with me."

Soldar followed the guard toward the door he had entered through. He stopped and looked over his shoulder. Ferrous was watching him leave, an inscrutable expression on his face. Soldar started to say something, then stopped. Ferrous was no longer the man he had known. He shook his head and continued walking alongside the guard. He had much to think about.

"A reluctant friend can be convinced."
~ Philaten, past Tamadar of the Sepharim


King Hamideh leaned forward in his saddle, almost flush with Flash's neck as they galloped through the forest, his hair plastered against his face. Riding Argothal was always a thrill, but being on the big sorrel horse was even more special. Flash was both his friend and equine partner, and their bond strengthened every day. He was so grateful to Rugal for gifting Flash to him at his coronation. Rugal had Tag, Johan had Raksh, and he had Flash. One thing all three young kings had in common was their love for their steeds.

Racing through the trees at a reckless speed, Hamideh kept Flash moving in the direction of King Nakasan's castle. Entering the courtyard, he was met by a member of the castle guard, a tall, muscular man in the green and yellow colors of

Arlesia, who grabbed Flash's reins as Hamideh dismounted. A young boy ran up and took the reins.

"I will see to your horse's comfort, sir," the lad gave a brief bow and led Flash toward the stable.

Hamideh faced the guard. "I need to see Mukatak and request an audience with King Nakasan."

The guard smiled. "We have been tracking you ever since you crossed our borders. Mukatak has invited you to join him for the midday day repast."

Hamideh nodded. He wasn't surprised. While *dynamis* did not exist in Arlesia, they had a highly developed infrastructure and were famous for efficient communication by training the birds that were common to their country. Smaller than flutebirds, they were stockier but with a similar wingspan. These birds, called banyars by the locals, frequented the forests surrounding the Arlesian capital. They did not have the same capacity for bonding with humans as flutebirds, but they were very intelligent in their own way. And highly trainable by those who understood them. Hamideh was quite sure he saw more than one winging overhead during his travels and wasn't surprised to be met by the castle guardsman.

The guardsman motioned toward the castle, and Hamideh unexpectedly found himself trembling slightly, his heart racing. He was no longer the boy playing pranks at court, he was the leader of Tolan. King Nakasan's response to his request would weigh heavily on their chances for success. He took a couple of deep breaths and reminded himself that he was King Hamideh, son of King Handerbin, and he had been trained thoroughly for such a moment as this. The words of the Swordsman came to mind.

*"True courage is to be afraid, and to overcome your fear."*

He could feel his trembling begin to subside. He gave a

brief nod and strode toward the castle's entrance, the guardsman following at a respectful distance.

MUKATAK'S SANDY HAIR, now streaked with grey, framed his wrinkled face. Flashing blue eyes directed at Hamideh, he shook his head, his jaw set. He looked down, splaying his fingers on the edge of the table, then looked back up and let out a noisy breath. "He won't do it. I think you know that."

"I know that Arlesia has a policy of keeping to itself. But I also know Arlesia desires peace," Hamideh returned, keeping his voice even. "I don't think you understand the magnitude of the situation."

"Tell me," Mukatak leaned forward.

"The words from the oracle impact all of us." Hamideh closed his eyes and began to recite the words that he would never forget. The words the Ring of Rosin spoke on the Day of Questioning during the Time of Sun Shadow, regarding the Neliphim that had attacked Rugal:

*He is evil beyond comprehension and possesses magic through his arrows. He and his people live across the sea. He will return and bring companions with the intent to destroy all of you. He is a Neliph, of the Neliphim clan...He is coming at the end of winter.*

Hamideh paused, his eyebrows knit with consternation and an unspoken pleading in his eyes.

"Was there any mention of Arlesia?" Mukatak shot back.

Hamideh's shoulders sagged. "No."

Mukatak straightened in his chair, tapping his fingers on the table's edge as he gazed into the distance, considering the young king's words. His brow creased as he mentally explored the implication of threat to Arlesia. Hamideh sat still, trying to keep from showing the anxiety he felt. He finally blew out a breath, and Mukatak refocused his attention on him.

"You are the only kingdom that has a fleet," Hamideh continued. "They are coming from across the ocean. With your ships, we would have a fighting chance." He bit his lip and looked down. "Without them, we will be at a huge disadvantage." He looked up and firmly met Mukatak's gaze. "One we may not be able to recover from."

"A compelling argument," Mukatak returned, his eyes narrowing. "But does not answer the question King Nakasan is sure to ask."

Hamideh's eyebrows rose in silent question.

Mukatak's voice held no emotion. "Why should we care?"

Before Hamideh could respond, the doors flew open, and a man dressed in castle livery burst into the room, stopping short of their table, breathing hard. Mukatak stood up and addressed the man. "What is it?"

The man, hand trembling, gave Mukatak a piece of paper. The insignia at the top indicated it had arrived via the Arlesian Avian Corps.

"One of the birds from our ocean outpost just brought this."

Mukatak looked down at the paper, frowning. He looked up and handed the paper to Hamideh, who had come around the table to stand at his side. Hamideh looked at the hurriedly scribbled note. The script was in Arlesian, and he quickly handed it back to Mukatak. "Forgive me, I know not what it says."

"It says..." Mukatak paused and took a breath. "Why we should care."

RUGAL SMILED at Farin in his brightly colored page attire, as he introduced the next petitioner. The young boy took his duties seriously and stood ramrod straight. He gestured to the farmer to move forward to the throne. The farmer's face was creased by a life in the sun and fields. His calloused hands clasped his hat and twisted it nervously as he approached the throne. Rugal leaned forward, doing his best to provide a reassuring presence. The business of the kingdom did not stop, despite the magnitude of what was looming over them, and today was court day.

Rugal, as all of the rightful kings of Elayas did before him, faithfully held to the tradition of being accessible to the citizens of Elayas, and today was no exception. Rugal's stomach gave a loud rumble, and he blushed a bright red that crawled up his cheeks. It was almost dinner time, and his stomach never failed to give his desire to be fed away. Rugal forcibly turned his thoughts to the man waiting patiently before him, seeming not to have noticed Rugal's contentious belly noises.

Rugal cleared his throat and gazed with a measure of affection at the man before him. "First of all, Farmer Talan, on behalf of the kingdom of Elayas, I would like to thank you for your service in the liberation of our country from Oldag's evil reign." Rugal glanced down at the paper in his hand, which contained background on each petitioner as well as the nature of their request for an audience. "I see you led the Patriotes in your village."

Farmer Talan met Rugal's eyes. "It was a privilege to be a part of the liberation, Sire. We are all grateful that you battled Oldag. His defeat changed everything."

Rugal nodded, the blush creeping back up his neck. "I could not have done so without the support of our people." He glanced down at the paper again. "It says here you also gave a portion of your crops to those in need, without charge. Fully fifty percent."

"Yes, Sire," Farmer Talan twisted his hat again. "I couldn't let our people go hungry."

Before Rugal could continue, the Swordsman stood up from where he often observed the court proceedings. All eyes swung toward him, and the big man put his hand over his heart. "The Sepharim thanks you, Farmer Talan." Jackal stood up next to him and bowed in Farmer Talan's direction.

Farmer Talan looked down, twisting his hat beyond recognition, his face flushing. "Twas nothing anyone else would have done," he muttered.

"Not so," Rugal replied firmly. "Farmer Talan," Rugal waited until the man looked back up at him.

"You have the gratitude of all Elayas. You have served above and beyond as a citizen of Elayas." He glanced at Jackal and the Swordsman and smiled, then returned his gaze to Farmer Talan. "I cannot grant your petition as it stands."

Farmer Talan jerked back, eyes wide with surprise, but before he could respond, Rugal continued. "I grant your petition for seed, which is the right of every citizen of Elayas as set up by King Rosin. In addition, in honor of your service to Elayas, I declare all debt owed to the crown for your land as paid in full. The ten-year promissory note has already been documented to reflect the new status, and," Rugal reached out to Farin, who hurriedly handed Rugal a piece of paper adorned with an elaborate script, "this is your certificate of ownership."

The weathered farmer dropped his hat in shock and moved his mouth but couldn't find words to speak. Rugal got up from his throne and embraced the older man. He whispered in his ear, "Without you and those like you, Farmer Talan, we would not be here today. You have selflessly shared the fruits of your labor. It is only fitting that you share in the result."

Rugal stepped back and took his seat, smiling broadly as Farmer Talan retrieved his hat. He bowed to the young man on the throne, his eyes moist. "Thank you, Sire," he managed, and allowed Farin to turn and guide him toward the throne room doors, the young page pausing for Rugal's permission to leave. Rugal inclined his head, and Farin and Farmer Talan continued out the doors.

"Well done," Jackal walked over to the throne and squeezed his son's shoulder.

"That's the best part about being a king," Rugal grinned. His stomach rumbled loudly again. "Good thing Farmer Talan was the last petitioner for today. Can we go eat now?" he asked plaintively. He glanced at Jackal with a small smile. "Lissa informs me Farathian cheese is on the menu for dinner today."

"What are we waiting for?" Jackal exclaimed. Rugal started to laugh, then paused and stared off into the distance. The beautiful lilt of Lissa's voice in his head was always breathtaking.

*How was court, my love? Did you get to see Farmer Talan today?*

*It was wonderful, dearest. Yes, I got to grant him his land today!*

*I can hear your happiness even in your thought voice. I am so proud of you. It's not often one can have the opportunity to reward someone so deserving in such a meaningful way.*

*I am so grateful you understand, my love. We are about to head for the dining hall.*

*That is why I reached out. I wanted to let you know that I can hear Argothal.*

*Is he alright?*

*Oh yes, he is carrying Dungellan. He will be joining us for dinner.*

*That's great news. I can't wait to introduce the Swordsman to Dungellan. Thank you, dearest.*

*Of course, my love. I shall see you soon.*

Rugal turned to his father. "Lissa can hear Argothal, so he must not be too far away. Dungellan will be joining us for dinner."

"Perfect timing," the Swordsman commented, joining them. They headed out the doors of the throne room together, their mood still light from the audience with Farmer Talan.

# CHAPTER
# TEN



*Learn from the past, to establish the future.*
~ Kargolith Proverb

Sharing the same huge stature as the Swordsman, Dungellan sat awkwardly astride the massive dragon, gripping Argothal's scales tightly as he peered down at the forests surrounding the castle. For the tenth time, he wished Johan could have accompanied him, but he understood the need for the leader of the Kargoliths to stay behind and organize their preparations for the upcoming battle. The end of winter would arrive soon enough, and Rohan was still at the Sepharim school learning how to use his *dynamis*.

Kargoliths were a fiercely independent people, and the council needed strong leadership. Superb horsemen, many Kargoliths continued their nomadic lifestyle despite the fact that they were now a recognized kingdom with their own territory. By remaining in Kargolith, Johan could unite their forces, and Kargolith, Elayas, and Tolan would be able to fight effectively under the same banner. The three kingdoms would present a much more formidable force than if each stood alone. The seasoned warrior let out a breath. Hopefully King Hamideh's efforts with the Arlesians would be successful. From Johan's description of the enemy, they would need all the help they could get.

A figure skulking about the trees surrounding the castle interrupted the thoughts running through Dungellan's head. From his vantage point on Argothal, he could see the person through gaps in the overhead foliage and watched the figure surreptitiously moving toward the castle. As Argothal flew nearer, a quiver of arrows on the figure's back sent alarms through Dungellan's mind. It was the wrong time of day for hunting. "Argothal, would you mind landing me near the side of the castle?" Dungellan found himself saying out loud.

Argothal tilted his head toward Dungellan, his eye changing color to a greenish hue from its usual yellow, the pupil spinning. He changed his trajectory, and Dungellan drew a sigh of relief. The dragon understood his request. He gripped his sword and tensed, readying himself to jump off the huge beast.

The person moving furtively through the forest had not noticed a huge dragon in the sky due to the cover of tree foliage, but now that they were flying over the castle grounds, they were in plain sight. At this closer vantage point, Dungellan could tell the figure was a young man carrying a bow. He was dressed in the simple clothes of a woodsman. Looking up in shock, the young man turned to flee back into the forest. Argothal glided in as close as he could to the running figure, and Dungellan leapt from the dragon's back, his sword held firmly in his hand. He somehow managed to land on his feet and sheathing his sword, Dungellan ran toward the young man, catching up to him as he was entering the shelter of the trees. He tackled him from behind, and the young man's bow flew through the air as they rolled on the ground, scattering the fallen leaves littering the forest floor.

Getting to his feet, Dungellan pulled the young man up with him and turned him so he could see his face. The young man looked back, his eyes wide and his scrawny body trembling. "Please, sir, let me go," he managed in a quaking voice. "I mean no harm."

Dungellan loosened his grip, but only slightly. "That is not what it looks like on the surface, lad. Why were you skulking about the castle with a bow and quiver of arrows?"

At the mention of his bow, the young man looked frantically around and relaxed when he spotted it. "I am a simple woodsman, sir," the young man replied. "I made the bow and arrows so that I could hunt food for myself." He squirmed in the huge man's grasp. "May I get my bow?"

Initially shocked at the young man's audacity, Dungellan paused, then laughed. "For someone who was just caught skulking about the king's castle, you are indeed bold. Who are you?"

Before the young man could answer, Rugal, Jackal, Mura, and the Swordsman came riding up on their horses. Rugal looked down from his mount at Dungellan. "Argothal informed Lissa of your unexpected dismount." He turned his gaze to the gaunt youth. "And who is this?"

At that moment, Finn came charging up on foot. "Kenrik," she gasped. She shoved Dungellan aside and embraced the youth, who wrapped his arms around Finn in return.

"I thought you were dead," she said in a strangled voice.

"That was the general idea," Kenrik replied, laughing.

Finn stepped back and shook her head in confusion. "What are you doing here?"

"I came to find you."

"You are telling me the leviathan rescued you when you fell into the sea?" Finn shook her head in disbelief. "But I thought it was entrapped by Frakar."

"She is," Kenrik agreed. "Against her will. But there is a short window every few days, when her mind returns to her own control. I think it has to do with Frakar's *dynamis* needing to be revitalized. It must be quite a drain to maintain that level of control over such a huge creature." He paused, gathering his thoughts. "She saved me. I was testing out a hull I had been working on when a sudden storm blew up. Before I knew it, the sea was raging all around me." He closed his eyes as if reliving the dreadful memory. "I was swept off the bow and into the sea. I couldn't keep my head above water, and it was too dangerous for anyone else to jump in and try to save me. I thought I would surely drown, but that is when the leviathan rescued me.

"I was sinking rapidly, a current pulling me down, when she came alongside me and turned her gaze upon me. I somehow knew in that moment that she wanted to help me. I grasped one of her scales and held on for dear life." He opened his eyes. "I am not sure what happened after that, but I woke up on a nearby island."

Kenrik gazed at Finn in wonder. "I have managed to befriend her. I can even communicate with her in my head sometimes. She has a very sad story. Her service to Frakar keeps her in constant sorrow. She misses her mate." He frowned, putting his hand to his throat. "Just as much as we have been miserable in our captivity, so has she."

Finn shook her head in amazement. "So, she is a girl? I never considered her feelings. And I can't believe you followed me here. How did you get here?"

"I asked the female leviathan for help. After you must have already left on Frakar's ship, the leviathan's mate came to the island. He brought me here."

Finn looked at him in disbelief, but he held out his hands.

"It's true. I lived on the island for several weeks. Eventually, the female leviathan asked him to come help me. I fashioned a rope from some vines I found on the island and tied it around his neck. I held on tightly while he swam across the ocean to bring me here." His eyes widened. "He has some kind of magic, Finn. He travels at an unbelievable speed through the waves." He paused. "But enough about me. I can't believe you managed to stow away on Frakar's ship." He looked at her with some consternation. "I wish I had been there to help."

"I thought you were dead, remember? And I couldn't have hidden us both. My *dynamis* will only hide me. I had to do this."

Kenrik gazed affectionately back at the red-haired young woman standing jauntily in front of him. "You are right," he laughed, then his expression turned serious. "I was worried about you."

Finn looked down and smiled shyly. She picked up his bow that lay on the ground nearby where he'd dropped it. Running her fingers along the wood, she nodded her head in approval. "Nice work."

Kenrik beamed. "I was glad to have the opportunity to create something for my own use rather than working on ships for Frakar's evil intentions."

Finn stiffened, remembering her own servitude, assigned to care for the trees planted for the timber that would eventually find its way into Kenrik's skilled hands. "How much is left to be done in the shipyards?"

"Not as much as I would like, but my disappearance will have slowed Frakar's progress somewhat."

"That's good news."

Everyone waited patiently during this initial exchange, and finally, the Swordsman looked down at both of them with a grin. "Finn, aren't you going to introduce us?"

Finn blushed, realizing the king of Elayas and his most trusted counselors were sitting on their horses, waiting for them to finish their conversation. She turned and did a quick curtsy.

"Sire, may I introduce you to my betrothed, Kenrik."

She elbowed Kenrik, and he gave a hurried bow while Finn continued, "I am pleased to introduce you to Rugal, the King of Elayas; his mother, Mura; his father, Jackal," she paused, her smile widening, "and my uncle Zander, also known as the Swordsman." She turned toward Dungellan, who had remained off to the side observing the proceedings. "And you must be Dungellan, since your arrival upon Argothal was expected today."

Dungellan nodded his agreement.

"Thank you, Finn," Rugal inclined his head. "Let us continue this in the castle," he suggested. "It seems we have much to talk about."

"You are a shipbuilder by trade?" Jackal leaned forward in his chair. The group had transitioned to the library, and a fire was hastily lit to chase away the evening chill that would be descending soon.

Kenrik had been staring into the flames and jerked his attention back to the people scattered about the large table in its center.

He cleared his throat and straightened up in his seat. "Yes, I was on the work crew assigned to build the ships for the Neliphim's fleet. The supervisor is an Arlesian master ship-builder, kidnapped by Frakar a few years ago. Landan is his name. The Arlesians think he was lost at sea. We took the timber that was grown and processed by Finn's crew and worked it into the forms needed to build the hulls." He bowed his head, his voice choking. "We didn't want to, but we had no choice." He sniffed. "Our families would have suffered if we refused."

Finn came around the table and wrapped her arms around Kenrik's shoulders, letting her tears fall. Every eye in the room grew moist at the scene. Finally, Rugal spoke up.

"Do not trouble yourself with those thoughts, Kenrik. You and Finn did the right thing. You protected your family and your village."

Kenrik met Rugal's gaze and wiped the tears from his eyes with the back of his hand. Finn loosened her hold around his shoulders but remained, resting a hand on his arm. She smiled gently at Kenrik. "You have always been honorable. Do not torture yourself. You and I are here now, and we can help."

A look of determination came over the young man's face. "Yes, we can." He turned his gaze to Rugal. "Sire, I know how many ships the Neliphim have, but even more, I know their vulnerabilities. I would be glad to share that information with you."

Rugal nodded, smiling. "We would greatly appreciate that knowledge, Kenrik. It could help turn the tide."

The others looked puzzled as the young shipbuilder started

laughing in return. Finally, Kenrik shook his head, still grinning. "Tide," he gasped. "Ships...tide..."

Rugal chuckled, and Finn gazed affectionately at her betrothed. "These are good people, Kenrik. We're going to be okay."

Kenrik looked at the people gathered around. "Thank you. I will help in any way I can." His face grew solemn, with a glimmer of pain in his eyes. "The Neliphim are evil, and they have no mercy. Their fleet can easily carry two thousand or more. They are a formidable foe. Darkness is coming to your lands."

CHAPTER

# ELEVEN

"We must never give up hope for a better future."
~ Mura

The morning sun was emerging over the distant meadows, its rays breaking through the foliage of the trees, when the Swordsman sauntered down to the practice yard. Yesterday had been filled with the startling revelations brought by Kenrik, and he felt the need for direct action to relieve the stress he was feeling. He began scanning the area in hopes of finding a practice partner, when Dungellan emerged from the castle entrance. The Kargolith warrior took a deep breath of the morning air and looked around, his sword in its sheath at his side.

The Swordsman, smiling broadly, waved his arms in the air. "Hello, Dungellan, over here!"

Dungellan wheeled in the Swordsman's direction, his hand on his sword hilt. Seeing it was the Swordsman who called out, he relaxed and started to walk toward the practice yard. He entered the dirt arena, but before he could speak, the Swordsman raced toward him, sword drawn.

"AAAAAAAAAAAEEEEEE!" the Swordsman bellowed at the top of his lungs. Dungellan hastily drew his sword as the huge man approached and managed to parry the blow the Swordsman doled out as he stepped into Dungellan's space. Dungellan raised his own sword and, springing to one side, held it ready.

"What are you doing?" Dungellan gasped. "I thought we were on the same side!"

"We are!" The Swordsman grinned as he barreled forward for another attack. He raised his sword in an offensive pose and met Dungellan's eyes. "If I am going to hand my guardsmen over to you while I am gone, I must know your mettle."

His eyes dawning with comprehension, the Kargolith warrior nodded. "Yes," he raised his sword. "I would do the same in your place."

With that, he lowered his sword slightly and charged the Swordsman. The two men fought evenly, blow for blow, as the sun crept higher into the sky. Time seemed to stand still, and a crowd of onlookers soon formed around them. They continued to fight, both men matching stroke for stroke.

"Gah, Swordsman, what's taking you so long?!!" Jackal called out, laughing.

"Dungellan, I thought you would have taken him by now," Rugal added.

Both combatants turned and glared at their hecklers and resumed fighting. First, one, then the other, would press the advantage, but neither seemed to completely overcome the other. The practice yard rang with steel on steel. The Swordsman grunted and launched another flurry, which

Dungellan managed to deflect. Finally, he lowered his sword and grinned. "You hungry?"

Dungellan lowered his sword and grinned back. "Yes."

"Good," he sheathed his sword. "Let's go eat lunch."

Dungellan sheathed his sword too, and the two huge men walked side by side, ignoring the crowd, toward the castle.

"I guess Dungellan passed," Jackal breathed to Mura.

Mura laughed and grabbed his hand. "I would say so. I don't think I have seen a swordfight go on for so long. I think our troops will be in excellent hands."

Jackal nodded, chuckling. "I think you are correct, my lady." Something impinged on his senses, and he looked up at the sky. A bird was winging toward them. "It seems Treble is returning with news from King Hamideh." He turned to include Rugal in the conversation. He pointed skyward. "We'd best get back to the castle."

SEATED near the fire in the castle's informal dining room, Rugal carefully unfolded the note that had been attached to Treble's leg. Settled on his customary perch, Treble was busy preening his wings, having gulped down the tasty mash Rugal set before him when he first arrived. Melad had sent lunch, and the table boasted simple but hearty offerings of meat and Farathian cheese. The smell of freshly baked bread made each person salivate with anticipation, and everyone fell to serving themselves. It was hard to tell which plate was piled higher—the Swordsman's or Dungellan's, after their hours-long expenditure of energy.

Lissa, seeing Rugal occupied, selected Rugal's favorites from the table and set his plate beside him.

Rugal looked up with a grateful smile. "Thank you, dearest."

Lissa smiled in return and brushed back his hair from his eyes with a gentle hand, then returned to the table to get her own plate. Soon Lissa, along with Jackal, Mura, the Swordsman, and Dungellan, were seated, and fell to their meals. Janar slipped into the dining hall and, with a quick smile and a wink, walked over to the food table and made his selections, joining everyone at the table. Finn and Kenrik, taking a gentle hint from Mura that perhaps they could picnic during the meeting, were absent.

Jackal snuck a piece of cheese off of Mura's plate and popped it into his mouth. He took a sip of his ale, wiped his mouth with the back of his hand, then gazed expectantly at his son.

Rugal looked up at his father and grinned. "It's a most interesting letter." He looked down and cleared his throat. The room became very still as those chewing hastily swallowed their bites. He began to read:

*Greetings King Rugal,*

*I have successfully made contact with the Arlesians. I must thank you again for such a fine steed. Flash carried me swiftly and faithfully on my mission. Why, even King Nakasan asked if he could buy Flash. Of course, my answer was no.*

*They were initially reluctant to join us in our effort to come together against the Neliphim, but whilst I was talking with Mukatak, the king's advisor, a message arrived. The Arlesians have a type of bird that carries messages for them, much like Treble does for you. What is remarkable is that these ordinary birds are trained to fly between locations and provide a reliable network that is always available. I can see their use in the upcoming war, if King Nakasan would be willing to loan us some of them.*

*The message brought by the bird contained news of one of their ships not far from shore being attacked and destroyed by a leviathan. Witnesses on the beach spoke of a foreign ship approaching the Arlesian vessel. When they were close enough, a man from the foreign ship boarded the Arlesian vessel, and they could see him talking to the captain on the forward deck. The discussion looked heated as the Arlesian shook his head vigorously, refusing whatever request the foreigner was making.*

*The foreigner returned to his own ship and signaled for his crew to steer away from the Arlesian vessel, but not before something strange happened. The foreigner turned toward the sea and pulled out a whistle, which he brought to his mouth, blowing a series of notes on it. The sound carried across the water, which the witnesses on the beach heard. After the foreign ship was a good distance away, the sea erupted, and a giant sea creature attacked the Arlesian ship. In minutes, both ship and crew vanished into the ocean.*

Rugal paused, eyebrows wrinkled. "A giant sea creature fighting on behalf of the Neliphim? That is not good news." He looked back down at the letter. "Hmmm, Hamideh goes on to say that is why the Arlesians agreed to help. So, while the destruction of the ship is terrible, it was also a catalyst for the Arlesians to see it is in their best interests to join us." He shook his head. "I hate that it happened, but I am thankful to know we can leverage the Arlesian fleet in our efforts to overcome the Neliphim."

"Yes," Jackal agreed. "We can be grateful when we find good even in the midst of bad things." His eyes softened. "I grieve the loss of life, but I never would have gotten my Mura if it wasn't for those marauders attacking the caravan. She was unreachable for someone of my station, but dire circumstances brought us together."

Rugal smiled affectionately at his birth parents. "I must admit I am very grateful you found each other."

Everyone laughed, and Rugal paused, allowing them to enjoy the moment. "Thank you, Father. I think that is excellent advice. It is good to remind ourselves in times of trouble that we can often draw some good from every situation. It can be very hard to see, especially in the midst of it, but I can also look back and see where difficult times in my own life turned out to my good or allowed me to help someone else going through something similar."

He held up the letter. "King Hamideh also mentions that an Arlesian master shipbuilder disappeared about five years ago and was never seen again. No one knows why or what happened to him. Mukatak suspects he may have been kidnapped by the Neliphim."

Rugal leaned back, his eyes contemplative. "I am amazed at the long-range plans of our enemy. Growing a forest of timber that takes twenty years to mature so they can use the wood to build a fleet to attack us." He shook his head. "Kidnapping people to forward their plans. He must be the Arlesian master shipbuilder Kenrik mentioned. And now, kidnapping Soldar. It's hard to fathom." The room grew quiet as each person reflected on Rugal's words.

"There is evil in the world," Janar spoke up, "and it never sleeps." Much to Jackal's delight, his mentor had remained at court in an advisory capacity. Janar's years of experience and wisdom were invaluable. The stocky older man's expression in his brown, wrinkled face tightened. "Evil will go to any lengths to defeat good."

Janar swept back his grey hair and abruptly stood up, his eyes flashing. He banged his fist on the table, rattling the food on his plate. "We must not allow evil to overcome us!" He sat back down and glanced at Rugal, and his voice softened. "Just as we fought Oldag, we must fight the Neliphim. The risk is great, but the alternative is..." he paused and blew out a noisy breath. "The alternative is too horrendous to think about."

"Indeed," the Swordsman agreed. "We must never forget why we fight. We are not trying to gain land or treasure. We are not even fighting just to defend ourselves, although," he gave a grim smile, "that is certainly motivating." He met Janar's eyes and nodded. He turned back to the others. "We are fighting to rid our lands of evil."

Jackal raised his mug of ale, "To defeating evil!"

Everyone raised their mugs in response. "To defeating evil!" chorused from every throat.

Rugal looked around his table of family and trusted friends who were like family. He smiled, and his face set with determination. "The oracle of the Ring of Rosin told us that the future is cloudy and there are no assurances. The road ahead is difficult and uncertain, but there is no one I would rather have by my side than each of you." He glanced at the letter in his hand. "Now that we know we have the support of the Arlesians, I think we'd best have a strategy meeting." He turned to the Swordsman.

"Are you still planning on embarking on a spy mission with Finn and Legas in the morning?"

"Yes, Sire," he hesitated a moment. "And perhaps Kenrik. Argothal is capable, and it may be helpful to have someone familiar with their ships along."

Rugal nodded. He had not quite let go of his desire to accompany them, but he understood the necessity of his staying in Elayas. Being king was certainly not getting to do what one wanted, but rather, doing what was best for the kingdom. A burden he felt heavily at times. "Yes, that seems to be a good idea." He scratched his head, glanced at Dungellan, and then back to the Swordsman. "I have shared all of the relevant parts of Hamideh's note. Let's adjourn for now and meet this evening. That will give you and Dungellan the opportunity to coordinate your strategy for our guardsmen before you leave in the morning."

"Yes, Sire," voices chorused around the table.

Mura looked pointedly at a second piece of paper that Rugal had not referenced that he was still holding.

Rugal grinned. "Nothing to do with our plans, Mother. It appears to be a note from Princess Gillian to Yandin."

Mura smiled. "Now that is good news. Even in the midst of war, life does go on. We must never give up hope for a better future."

Rugal returned his mother's smile. "Yes, you taught me that." He glanced around the table. "All of you. That is why we are here today." He turned to Lissa, stood up, and held out his arm. "Shall we go for a walk, my lady?"

Eyes bright, Lissa stood up and put her arm in his, and they walked out the doors of the dining hall.

CHAPTER

# TWELVE

"If you fail to plan, you plan to fail."
~ The Swordsman

"**W**hat does the note to Yandin say?" Lissa asked breathlessly, her eyes alight with curiosity.

Rugal paused and chuckled. "Now, Lissa, it's a private note to Yandin. It is our job to deliver it, not read it."

Lissa let out an exasperated sigh. "You are right, of course." She perked up. "I saw him earlier at the swordfight. He must be around."

Rugal nodded, smiling. "Yes, he is on the castle grounds. He came back from visiting his family in Regos yesterday. I wager we will be able to find him in the stables."

Lissa started trotting down the path, dragging Rugal with

her, their laughter ringing through the courtyard. Coming to the stable area, they slowed to a walk.

"There he is," Lissa pointed at a sandy-haired figure brushing down one of the castle horses.

Yandin heard Lissa's voice and turned around, his dark brown eyes taking in their appearance, and his gaze drawn to the note in Rugal's hand. "Greetings, Sire, my Lady," Yandin hastily gave a half bow and attempted to brush his unruly hair into place.

"No need for formality," Lissa replied in a soothing voice. She smiled broadly at the young man. "It seems you have a message from Princess Gillian. It arrived by bird from King Hamideh. Treble brought it today."

The young man's eyes widened, and then his face broke into a shy grin. His hand trembled as he held it out to receive the note. Rugal placed it in his hand, and before either one of them could say anything else, Yandin grabbed it, turned around, and ran as fast as he could toward the hay loft.

"Well," Lissa harumphed. "I guess Yandin doesn't want to share his letter."

Rugal burst out laughing. "Well, would you, if you were in his shoes?"

Lissa blushed. "No. I would want to know what it said before I shared it." She sighed and glanced toward the hay loft. "I hope he tells us what she said."

Rugal winked at his beloved. "I am sure he will. If he decides to plan a trip to Tolan, he will have to arrange for his absence."

Lissa's face lit up. "Wouldn't that be wonderful?!!" She reached up and wrapped her arms around Rugal. "I want everyone to find their special someone. I am so glad you're mine!" She tilted her head toward his and gave him a kiss.

Rugal savored Lissa's sweet lips on his, then pulled back so he could look at her face. He reached up and put an unruly light brown curl back into place. "And I am so glad you're mine!"

"Is everyone ready?" Rugal looked around the table at the people gathered in the library to offer their wisdom and experience in building an effective strategy for the coming war. The Swordsman and Dungellan, sitting across from him, nodded sharply. Rugal looked first at Dungellan, then Finn and Kenrik. He spread out his hands. "When we are able, we begin our meetings with a simple ceremony." He gave a small smile. "It is good to remind ourselves who we are and what we have pledged our lives to. You do not need to be a member of the Sepharim to take part. Please feel free to observe and participate as you are comfortable." He turned to Tonar and grinned. "You know the ceremony as well as I do. Would you like to lead us?"

Tonar gasped, eyes wide. He drew in a breath to calm himself. "But I have no *dynamis*," he exclaimed.

Mura smiled affectionately at the young man who had come to be Rugal's best friend. "You have a heart to serve others, Tonar. You are loyal to the kingdom of Elayas. That is all that is required."

Jackal and Janar murmured their affirmation, and Lissa gazed affectionately at the young man who had sacrificed his own well-being for Rugal's sake during their journey to recover the Ring of Rosin. The fire from the wall sconces danced across the faces of the attendees as they waited patiently. Treble, looking alert on his customary perch, flapped his wings and gave an encouraging chirp.

"But, I…"

Rugal gently punched his friend in the shoulder. "No buts, Tonar. Please, do us the honor."

Tonar let out a long, noisy breath and, rubbing his palms together, he closed his eyes and began to recite the ancient words, which were engraved on his heart:

Seidous Sepharim alkalfam dous mosfet sandali.

*We pledge ourselves to the Sepharim and to each other.*

Seidous man shoma dynamis shod elis toujou keen.

*We pledge to use our powers for good and to defend against evil.*

Seidous azaram man Elayas khubay anax shod.

*We pledge our allegiance to the rightful king of Elayas.*

Seidous man dynamis ferilux Elayas, Tolan, des Kargolith anthropoi shod.

*We pledge our powers to defend the people of Elayas, Tolan, and Kargolith.*

"THIS IS A BEAUTIFUL MAP," the Swordsman leaned over it. "It's not the one we were using before. Where did you get it?"

"It arrived by courier just yesterday," Jackal spoke up. "It is a gift from Legas to the king of Elayas."

"Now I see why you want to take Legas with you," Rugal commented. "He does excellent work."

"Exactly," the Swordsman agreed. "Dungellan, if you please," he gestured toward the huge man. "I want to show you where I think we should position our guardsmen." He ran his finger from Cargoa down toward the lake that fed into the Selba River. "Our troops have been training on swordplay ever since Rugal's coronation." He looked up. "We should leave a contingent of swordsmen to guard the castle and move the rest here."

"Why there?" Rugal asked, eyebrows raised.

Dungellan held up his hand toward the Swordsman. "May I?"

The Swordsman gave Dungellan a piercing look, then nodded.

The big man dipped his head in acknowledgment and then turned to Rugal. "We need to split our forces so that we can protect the castle while being able to mobilize quickly to defend any threat coming from the south—from the Argonean Sea." He pointed to the map. "By placing our forces at the lake feeding into the Selba River," he moved his hand along the river and downward, "they will be able to spread out and head to the southern coast fairly quickly by boat." He shifted his hand toward the right side of the map. "Or if the enemy approaches Cargoa from the east, they will be able to pivot toward that direction. They can even split if the enemy comes from both directions." He paused and glanced over at the Swordsman. "Am I missing anything?"

The Swordsman grinned. "Not a thing." He slapped Dungellan on the back. "It seems we think alike. I won't have to worry while I'm on the spy mission."

"I'll do my best," Dungellan replied. "We have a sound strategy."

"In addition to other forces," Rugal spoke up. "We'll have archers from Tolan and, of course, your warrior horsemen from Kargolith."

He reached over and ran his finger from Tolan toward Arlesia. He was wearing the Ring of Rosin, a habit he had fallen into after it had been stolen, and he had recovered it. Its significance as an oracle made him reluctant to risk it being away from his person. The ring unexpectedly began to glow, and the map underneath his hand also began to glow and to shimmer.

Dungellan jumped back as the map coalesced into a new version that showed all of their troop placements on it. Rugal's castle guard was plainly evident in the form of men holding swords in front of the castle on the map. Archers were shown in front of King Hamideh's castle in Tolan. Horsemen were scattered about the Kargolith territory.

"What happened?" Rugal withdrew his hand and turned toward the Swordsman. The map shimmered and returned back to its original state.

The Tamadar grinned. "Now I know why Legas chose to be a cartographer. It seems his *dynamis* works well with his chosen profession." He raised his hand gently in a calming gesture. "It looks like Rugal triggered what Legas had implanted in the map. It responded to the Ring of Rosin."

"This is a tremendous advantage," Jackal breathed. "I wonder, will it show troop movements as they occur?"

"Easy enough to test," the Swordsman replied. He walked over to a window facing the practice yard and peered down. Spying one of his guardsmen, he bellowed, "Candar, run as fast as you can to the forest's edge. Once you reach it, you may return and go about your duties."

The young man looked up at the Swordsman and nodded, a puzzled look on his face, then took off at a run.

"Candar is a good soldier," Dungellan observed.

"Yes," the Swordsman replied, his eyes alight with pride. "He has at least two hundred yards to go. Let's see what happens." He pointed toward the map, and Rugal placed his hand with the ring upon it a second time. The map shimmered in response, and when it resolved into its new version of showing troops, this time, they could see one of the men moving westward, away from the castle, toward the forest edge.

"Amazing!" Jackal slapped the Swordsman on the back. "A tremendous gift from Legas. That will be very useful." He paused, thinking. "I wonder if we will be able to see enemy troops on the map."

"I have no idea," the Swordsman admitted. "Legas might not even know, since this is new territory for all of us." He turned back to Dungellan, who had resumed his place at the table. "I'll introduce you to the troops in the morning before I leave."

Dungellan nodded. "I'm looking forward to it." He met the Swordsman's gaze. "Don't worry. I will take care of your men as if they are my own, while you are away."

The Swordsman nodded. "That's all I can ask for."

Rugal stood up and stretched, then pointed back at the map. "We still need to develop a strategy for the Tolan archers and Kargolith horsemen and designate the framework we will be using to communicate between our troops."

"Correct, Sire," Janar spoke up, his weathered face serious as he contemplated the map. "We can't allocate troop positions until we know the enemy's position. It will be critical to have communications in place so that information can be rapidly disseminated and acted upon."

Rugal crossed his arms. "That is where Tonar, along with Lissa and Mura, come in." He glanced at his friend. "Tonar will be in charge of a central command post, that will enable him to either use Treble to carry a message or send riders to our various outposts as needed. The Patriotes already have a vast network he can tap into."

Tonar cleared his throat and turned to Dungellan. "I would also ask for some of the Kargoliths to take part. Your superb horsemen and fast horses could play a vital role in keeping our troops informed."

Dungellan scratched his head. "I am sure we can accommodate your request. I will need to send a message to King Johan."

"Certainly," Rugal replied. "We can ask Treble to oblige in getting a message to him." He turned toward Lissa and Mura. "And you both have a very important task. We need to set up a network that can send fire signals along the southern and eastern beaches. It will be critical to locate the enemy and send information regarding their movements when they arrive on our coast."

He smiled at Lissa. "I have arranged for twelve castle guardsmen to accompany you. They will be able to set up the beacons." Rugal paused. "And I will feel better knowing both of you are being accompanied by seasoned troops."

Mura's eyebrows rose, and she shot a glance at her son.

"Yes, Mother, I have heard the story of you and Father when your caravan was attacked, and you fought off a pack of gormalins. I know you are capable. But I will still feel better."

Jackal gently squeezed Mura's shoulders, and she relaxed. "I'll enjoy traveling with Lissa and the guardsmen," she admitted. "They will be of great assistance."

"Treble will also be available to you. It may be challenging, but between you and Tonar, we should be able to communicate with our troops." He smiled affectionately at Lissa. "And you'll be communicating with me, of course." He looked at the familiar faces around him. "Anything else?"

After a momentary silence, the Swordsman spoke up. "I think we are in a good place, Sire. Perhaps it is best to adjourn. Finn, Kenrik, and I will be leaving on Argothal in the morning to pick up Legas and head to the Neliphim lands. Tomorrow will be a busy day."

Rugal inclined his head. "Thank you. See you all tomorrow." He walked over and held his arm out for Lissa, and the two led the way toward the doors exiting the library.

*It's getting real, isn't it?* Rugal never tired of hearing Lissa's voice in his head, even when the topic was unpleasant.

*Yes, it is, dearest.* Rugal replied.

*Are you scared?*

Rugal stopped for a moment and took a deep breath. *Yes.*

*So am I.*

*It will be okay. I believe that.*

*I believe that, too.*

*So, why are you scared?*

*The unknown is always scary. The Ring of Rosin said the future is not assured.*

*We have each other. Isn't that enough?*

*I thought so when we first met. But not anymore. I must also keep our people safe. It's not just about us.*

Lissa stopped and pulled away from Rugal so she could look him in the eyes, hers shining with compassion and love.

"I know," she whispered.

CHAPTER

# THIRTEEN

*Where there is no try, there is no chance.*
~ Old Selban Saying

"Down there!" The Swordsman leaned over to the right and quickly grasped the scale in front of him as Argothal responded to his direction. He looked down and checked his compass. "Just like you said, Finn," the Swordsman glanced behind him, approval in his voice.

Finn glowed under her uncle's praise and Kenrik reached over from his position behind her and gave her shoulder a gentle squeeze. Legas, seated behind Kenrik on the back of the massive dragon, observed the two in front of him, a smile playing about his mouth. It was good to see love blossoming even in dire circumstances. How they managed under the servitude of the Neliphim was a testament to the resiliency of the human spirit. He shook his head. Interesting, too. Finn possessed *dynamis*. Kenrik did not, yet he was one of the most resourceful people Legas had ever met. Once they got through all of this, and he breathed to himself, *We will—somehow!* It would be interesting to see what they would accomplish together.

Argothal began his descent toward the island the Swordsman indicated. The sun was setting, and they would have to hurry if they wanted to set up camp while there was still some daylight. All of the humans tightened their grasp on Argothal's scales as he backwinged onto the island, settling into its sandy surface. The Swordsman jumped off and awkwardly stroked the scales on the dragon's chin. "Thank you, Argothal." He reached out his hand and helped Finn clamber down Argothal's foreleg. Finn ran to the front of Argothal, arms outstretched and red hair in disarray. The dragon dipped his head, and Finn wrapped her arms around it in a hug.

Kenrik and Legas had clambered down after her, and Legas playfully elbowed Kenrik in the ribs. "Looks like you have some competition," he grinned.

Kenrik, his eyes glued to Finn, laughed in return. "I think having a dragon for a friend can only be an advantage."

Legas chuckled. "I think you are right."

"We'd best make camp," the Swordsman looked around and gestured toward a stand of trees further up the beach. "That place looks as good as any."

Kenrik and Legas pulled their packs off of the dragon's back, and they started trudging to the area the Swordsman indicated. The long ride left them somewhat sore, and it was good to be walking again. The next day's journey promised to be just as long, and they were eager to set up camp and recover from this day's travel. Argothal flapped his wings and waddled off to a section of beach to his liking and curled up in the sand.

"Doesn't he need to eat something?" Finn asked the Swordsman anxiously as she watched her massive friend close his eyes, his long tail wrapped around his body.

"No," the Swordsman assured her. "I talked to Ethiod before we left. He said that Argothal eats a large meal every few days, and he ate right before we left. He will be fine."

Satisfied, Finn joined the others in making camp. The Swordsman used his *dynamis* to weave a strand of protection around the group so that he would know if danger approached, and soon they were all asleep under the stars.

RUGAL GRINNED AT YANDIN. He had wandered down to the stable on the pretext of checking on Tag, in hopes of running into him. The memory of a boy holding a rough-hewn sword, spooking Rugal's horse and charging him, swinging his sword wildly, came to mind. "How do you like being the royal black-smith, Yandin? I hear you have taken on additional duties as the stable master."

The young man looked down and blushed. "I like it lots, Sire. Seemed only natural, taking it on. Already being around the horses and all."

"I could not ask for a better man," Rugal reached out and put his hand on Yandin's shoulder. "You are doing a fine job."

Yandin ducked his head, his face glowing. Then he gathered his courage and looked back up, meeting Rugal's gaze. He straightened up and cleared his throat. "I have a request, Sire."

Rugal nodded, wishing to himself that Lissa was there. "Yes, Yandin?"

Yandin dug into his pocket and held out a well-worn letter. The crumpled paper indicated he had kept it on his person and had read it many times. "It's about the Princess Gillian," he muttered shyly.

"I see," Rugal replied. Accepting the letter, he carefully opened it and read the note written in elegant script. Eyebrows raised, he looked back at Yandin and waited patiently.

Yandin dug his hands in his pockets and looked back down. Finally, he mumbled, "Princess Gillian is royalty. I am a simple farm boy. How could this ever work?"

Rugal gestured to a bench, and they both sat down. Rugal looked at the boy who, in this past year, had finished his apprenticeship in a matter of months and had become the royal blacksmith—a testament to his courage, perseverance, and work ethic. "Why not," he asked gently.

"Because, uhhh," Yandin stuttered. He looked up at Rugal, tears in his eyes. "How can I ever do her justice. I come from Regos, a humble village, and she is the daughter of a king!"

Rugal leaned back against the bench and laughed. Yandin jerked his head around and glared at Rugal, then realized who he was glaring at and looked down instead. Rugal reached over and patted his knee. "Don't worry, Yandin, matters of the heart evoke strong emotions. I wasn't laughing at you. I was recalling someone else who was in a similar position."

Yandin's head popped back up. "Who?!"

Rugal smiled. "My parents. Jackal and Mura. My father came from Farath and was hired to be a caravan guard. That is how he met my mother, Mura. Did you know Mura is the cousin of King Rosin?"

"No, I didn't," Yandin gasped. "Actually, I didn't think about your lineage. I just assumed it must be royal since you fought and killed Oldag."

"Lineage is only one part of what makes a person," Rugal replied gently. "Your response to people is what defines you. You have shown yourself to be a loyal, hard-working man who cares for those around him. I don't think Princess Gillian could ask for a better man than that."

*Well done!!*

Lissa's unmistakable lilt echoed in his mind, and he paused.

*Where are you?*

*I am with Mura. We are discussing our travel plans.*

*I could have used your help here.*

Lissa laughed—she could hear Rugal's grumbling tone.

*You are doing fine, dearest.*

"Sire, did you hear me?"

Rugal shook his head. "Sorry about that, Yandin. I was momentarily distracted. What did you say?"

Yandin pointed to the letter. "What should I do?"

Rugal looked down at the letter in his hand and reread it.

*My brother, the king, trusts Lissa's judgment in this matter. Normally, he would request you travel to Tolan to become acquainted with myself and our family, but he understands the key role you have as the castle blacksmith in the upcoming war. He has granted permission for me to lodge in the castle under Lady Mura's guardianship and Lissa as my companion, if that is acceptable to them and you. He is asking you to respond in one week's time, so that you have time to seek counsel and examine your feelings. If this is acceptable, King Hamideh will arrange my transport. He is requesting Treble to return, with your response.*

Rugal looked back up and gazed at Yandin. "Put aside the obstacles you have already mentioned. What does your heart tell you?"

Yandin returned Rugal's gaze. "How does one know how one feels about someone they have never met? I do not know. Lissa thinks we would be a good match, and Princess Gillian is willing to meet me. If I don't at least try, I'll wonder for the rest of my life if I made a mistake."

Rugal nodded. "I agree. I think you should at least meet her." He paused and gazed off into the distance. "Love is a funny thing. It can happen quickly, but it becomes really special with the passage of time. My love for Lissa grows each day."

*Awww, thank you dearest. My love for you does as well.*

Rugal smiled. *You're still there?*

*Of course! I wouldn't miss this. You did good!*

Rugal blew out a noisy breath and focused back on the young man sitting next to him. He reached out and patted his leg. "Why don't you write your response, and we'll send it back."

Yandin, smiling shyly, dug into another pocket in his jacket and held out a piece of paper. "I already did. I just didn't know if I would have the courage to send it."

Rugal read it and punched Yandin gently in the arm. "Well done. Let me inform Mura since she will need to be designated as Gillian's guardian. We already know Lissa's answer—she will be thrilled." He paused in thought. "Gillian may need to accompany Mura and Lissa when they travel down south to coordinate the signal fire corps."

Yandin nodded. "I understand. When the time comes, we must all respond in the best interest of our people."

Rugal smiled affectionately at the young man. "That is something I admire about you, Yandin. You are a fine young man. I think Gillian will think so, too." He looked about and stood up. "Now I think I'll take Tag for a quick ride. I have a feeling the day is about to get very busy." Yandin jumped up and headed for the stable. "I'll have him right out for you," he called over his shoulder.

CHAPTER

# FOURTEEN

"Don't worry twice."
~ Lee, historian and teacher of Cargoa

Soldar paced the room, his brain whirring. It was exactly thirty-two steps from one wall to the other. For a man who relied heavily on using his intellect, he found it quite difficult to be stuck in a room with no means to pursue his scholarly studies. He had played the scene he had with Ferrous a hundred times in his mind but was no closer to finding a way to reason with him than when he first started. He gazed out the window and blew out a noisy breath in frustration. He brushed back his sparse brown hair and pushed his glasses farther up his nose. At least he was being fed, had the warmth of a fire when needed, and had a view of the castle grounds. But to what lengths would Ferrous be willing to go, to get the secret of the Key of Power?

Soldar scratched his head. He decided to follow the advice

of one of his teachers from so long ago, *Don't worry twice.* He walked over to the couch for an afternoon nap when he heard a knock on the door, then the lock disengaged. The young boy was back.

"Frakar requires your presence."

"I was wondering when he would," Soldar replied. "Lead the way."

Soldar followed the boy to another part of the castle. They came to a set of doors that opened into what amounted to be a private sitting area. A table and two chairs were placed near a fireplace. A tapestry created by Ferrous' father hung on one of the walls, a beautiful depiction of an armada of ships on the ocean. The ships were armed for battle and lightning bolts from the key King Rosin held skyward were striking an array of large mirrors—directing the lightning to the pirate ships, which were in flames. The boy indicated one of the chairs where Soldar should sit. "Frakar will be here soon," he said and left.

Soldar remained standing and walked over to the wall to study the tapestry, when he heard Ferrous' footsteps and turned around. "The colors are amazing. Your father was very talented."

"Yes." Ferrous walked up to the tapestry and gazed at it. "This was the first one he made. Before I was born."

Soldar studied the images on the tapestry carefully—directing his gaze at the markings on the ships. "It looks to be from the battle of the sea, early in King Rosin's reign. He is defending the southern shore from seafaring marauders."

"You are correct," Ferrous nodded. He turned to look intently at Soldar. "It depicts the mirrors King Rosin used to defeat the ships." He paused and reached out, rubbing his fingers along the tapestry's edge. "Using the Key of Power." He turned back to Soldar. "I have the box, you know."

"What box?" Soldar tilted his head, a questioning expression on his face.

"You know what box," Ferrous replied. "The one that accompanies the Key of Power."

"There is such a box?" Soldar asked, feigning ignorance.

Annoyance crept into Ferrous' voice. "You know there is a box. But it is useless without the Key of Power to open it." His face tightened. "I have it upstairs for safekeeping. I remembered your visits to King Rosin's chambers. When I told Magdarin of the artifacts you were cataloging for King Rosin—he took a special interest. Magdarin stole the box when he stole the tapestries my father had made for King Rosin and transported them all here."

Ferrous' voice softened. "I know you were caught by surprise. This can't be easy for you." He held a hand up in entreaty. "What is its secret?" A note of pleading entered his voice.

Soldar met his gaze, his mind racing. He needed to buy time. The more time Rugal had to prepare, the better off they would be. He looked back at the man who had been his best friend growing up. "Why do this, Frakar? You could enter into a treaty with Elayas, and we could all enjoy a mutually beneficial relationship."

Ferrous shook his head adamantly. "It's too late for that."

"That's unfortunate." Soldar sighed. "I'll think about it."

Ferrous' gaze hardened. He jerked back, and the edge returned to his voice. "Don't take too long."

"Try again," Vanjarli encouraged the Kargolith prince, who was the younger brother of Johan. "This time, take your time.

We will speed up your *dynamis* after you are comfortable wielding it effectively."

Rohan nodded. The slender young man with thick black hair and a dark, handsome face with lively eyes had become a favorite at the school. Having a Kargolith in their midst was exciting, and Rohan's paint horse, Jakash, was the envy of all. He gazed at his dark-haired classmate, Elgibran, who was walking slowly toward him.

Elgibran held up his arm, holding a stick as an imaginary sword. He broke into a slow trot and extended it, but when he got within a yard of Rohan, he froze, unable to move. Rohan reached out and grabbed the stick out of Elgibran's hand, and when he unfroze moments later, Rohan playfully tapped him with it. Both young men laughed and turned to see Vanjarli's response to Rohan's latest effort.

"Much better," Vanjarli's eyes gleamed, and he nodded his approval. He rubbed his cheek. "Is there any way you think you can extend the time your adversary remains frozen?"

Rohan stroked his chin, thinking. "When I see the need, I am able to control the timing for when they are immobile. It is almost instinctive. My *dynamis* just reacts. But I don't know how to hold it."

"Ah...that is very common," Vanjarli replied. "Most of us find our *dynamis* because a need arises, and we intuitively respond to that need with it. The challenge is learning how to control it effectively." He grinned at Rohan. "You have a great start. Now, I want you to try again. This time, when Elgibran approaches, think past your initial response. Focus on holding him in place."

Rohan nodded and tossed the stick back to Elgibran, who caught it easily and backed up so that Rohan could try again. "Beware, Kargolith prince," he called out. "Here I come to attack you!"

Elgibran began his approach, waving the stick about in a threatening manner. This time, Rohan stopped him handily and focused on keeping him immobile. His eyebrows scrunched together, and his jaw clenched with his effort. Elgibran stayed frozen for thirty seconds this time, before resuming his stance. Rohan, legs trembling with effort, looked to Vanjarli, who raised his fist and pumped it in victory.

"Well done, Rohan. I think you have the idea." The Sepharim master gazed intently at the young man. "Now, I think we need to speed things up regarding your attacker and teach you how you can replenish your *dynamis* when you feel drained. But enough for today." He looked approvingly at both young men. "Well done. Thank you for your assistance today, Elgibran."

The stout, dark-haired youth gave Vanjarli a quick half-bow. "It is my honor, Master Vanjarli. Rohan is a good friend."

Vanjarli clasped his hands, his expression serious. "Your friendship will stand you well in the coming days." He shook himself and grinned. "Now go, I hear they are serving Farathian cheese at lunch today. You best get there before it's all gone."

Rugal jerked awake, raising his head off of his pillow, his forehead sheening with sweat. He pulled back the blanket and jumped out of bed. He stood for a moment, trying to calm his rapid breathing, and quickly threw on some clothes. Treble awakened from his perch and flew to him. Rugal quietly opened the door to his bed chambers and slipped out. He padded silently down the hallway, Treble remaining quietly on his shoulder. He reached out with his mind.

*Lissa!*

*Hm...what...Rugal, are you okay?* Even Lissa's mental voice sounded sleepy.

*Yes, I mean no, I mean maybe.* He hesitated. *I had a bad dream.*

*Ohhh...I am sorry that happened.*

*Can you dress and meet me in the library? I'll build a fire.*

*Shouldn't you try to go back to sleep? You need your rest.*

*I don't think I can. I really want to talk about it.*

*Okay, I'll be right there.*

Reaching the library doors, Rugal entered, and Treble flew from his shoulder to the back of one of the chairs. He looked sleepily at Rugal, gave a little chirp, and tucked his head in the feathers of his wing, one eye peeking out at him. Rugal smiled affectionately at his feathered friend, then set about making a fire. The flames had just taken hold when Lissa entered, dressed and holding two cups of tea. She handed one to Rugal and sat in one of the chairs near the fire, allowing the heat to chase away the chill in the air, and took a sip of tea. Rugal sat down in another chair, holding his tea cupped in his hands. He looked at Lissa, who smiled gently at him.

"So, what happened?" Lissa asked encouragingly.

Rugal took a sip of the hot liquid, collecting himself. "It was very unexpected. It was also very scary."

Lissa looked at him in puzzlement. "Whatever could it be?"

"The giant sea creature," Rugal paused, and his eyes took on a faraway look. "The leviathan. She came and spoke to me in a dream." His eyes widened with sorrow. "I could feel her pain."

# FIFTEEN

*Family love is forever love.*
~ Dalbenian Saying

"What about Argothal?" Legas asked the Swordsman. The dragon had flown the last leg of their journey to the Neliphim lands in darkness and left them in a meadow large enough to accommodate his landing.

"He is going northward for a couple of days. Kenrik and Finn both agree that it's the safest place for him to wait. The lands north of the Neliphim are uninhabited."

Finn led the small band of spies through the forests of cultivated timber toward the compound where she and Kenrik had spent all of their lives. Peering through the trees, they could see the gates to the compound being patrolled by a pair of guards. The men sat on logs in front of a fire, playing some sort of game by tossing stones in a circle drawn in the dirt.

"They are always there," Finn whispered. "We need to circle around to the back of the compound. From there, we can enter through the secret entrance."

"Finn's right," Kenrik spoke up. "Once we are inside, we won't have to worry about being discovered. The Neliphim leave us alone unless we are out on a work detail."

Finn bounced up and down, barely able to contain her excitement. "You will get to see your parents, Uncle Zander!"

With Soldar's kidnapping, the need to spy on the enemy, and all of the logistics he must handle as Tamadar in the coming war, the realization that he was about to be united with his birth family had not fully registered. Once they had decided to fly to the Neliphim lands, he knew he would be able to see his parents, but something inside of him was afraid to acknowledge it. He had been wounded deeply by their disappearance and couldn't stand to be disappointed if they were no longer there.

He shook his head and smiled at his niece. With her disheveled hair and eyes wide with excitement, Finn reminded him so much of his younger sister, Zayla. "One thing at a time. First, we have to get into the compound undetected."

Finn stood still and peered curiously at the Swordsman, then nodded. They had all lost so much. She understood his feelings. Until it was real, it was safer not to get excited about it. "Sure, Uncle Zander." She turned and gestured to the others. "Crouch low and move as quietly as you can. The path is difficult to discern, but it is there. Once we get to the wall of the compound, we will be able to crawl through a tunnel to the inside."

FINN'S FAMILY hut was located toward the back of the compound, out of view of the guards at the front gate. Finn led the way to the front door and reached out a slender arm. She made a fist and knocked rapidly three times, then stepped back. The door opened, and a man stood in the doorway, bearing a faint resemblance to Finn.

His eyes widened, and he gasped, leaping forward and enfolding his daughter in his arms. Finn wrapped hers around him and buried her bright red head in his chest. He looked over her at the others standing awkwardly behind her and gently moved her back.

"Finn! You're home!" His voice dripped with gratitude. He peered at the figure standing closest to her, to one side. "Kenrik! We thought you were dead!" He stretched out an arm, and Kenrik moved forward. The two men hugged. "How did...who are?" Finn's father stuttered, his eyes moving from one person to the next.

Kenrik gave a rueful smile. "It's a long story." He paused, biting his lip. "I think best saved for another time."

"Well, the main thing is, you're here!" Finn's father replied, his eyes sparkling.

"Who's at the door?" a feminine voice called out from the hut's interior. The Swordsman froze, focusing on the tone. "It's late for visitors. Is everything okay?"

The Swordsman leapt forward and propelled himself past Finn's father. He peered inside the hut and strode toward the sound of his mother's voice. An older woman was looking through the doorway of a bedroom, a robe hastily thrown about her. She gazed anxiously at the figure coming toward her and hesitated, then let out a scream of joy, rushing out of the room and into her son's arms. The Swordsman wrapped his arms around his mother and picked her up off the floor in his excitement.

"Put me down, Zander," his mother laughed. The Swordsman obliged, and his mother looked up at him, cupping his chin. "My, how you've grown," she smiled, her eyes shining.

Before she could say another word, his father came into the room. He stopped a few feet from the Swordsman and drank in his son's presence with his eyes. He held out his hand and the Swordsman moved gently by his mother and grasped it. His father pulled him into a hug.

"I thought I would never see you again," he whispered.

"We can thank Finn for that, Father." He turned and grinned at his niece. "I didn't know what had happened to you and the others. She found me."

The Swordsman's father chuckled. "I am not surprised. She's spunky, just like your sister." He hesitated, and a shadow of sorrow crossed his face. "Do you know..."

"Yes, Father. Finn told me. I am so sorry."

"She missed you terribly," the Swordsman's mother spoke up.

"I missed her," the Swordsman replied, his voice choking. "I missed all of you." He closed his eyes and took a deep breath, blowing it out slowly. "But we are here together now. That is the important thing!"

"Yes," the Swordsman's mother agreed. She looked around. "Where are our manners? Come, come in, everyone. I'll put on some tea to warm you up, and you can tell us your plans and how we can help."

Finn's father nodded and gestured for Legas and Kenrik,

who had been watching the Swordsman greet his parents from the doorway, to enter the hut and join them.

THE HUT WAS QUITE CROWDED, but everyone found a seat, and the water began whistling merrily in its kettle. Finn moved about pouring tea for everyone. The Swordsman and Legas gave a summary of what had transpired in Elayas during their absence, and what the Swordsman hoped to accomplish while they were there in the lands of the Neliphim.

"You have done well, son," the Swordsman's father gazed upon him with pride. "Tamadar," he puffed out his chest a bit. "My son."

The Swordsman's mother playfully tapped his chest with her hand. "Now, now, 'tis his accomplishment, not yours," she chided her husband affectionately.

"That's not necessarily true, Mother," the Swordsman smiled. "Father did help me discover my *dynamis* and helped me learn how to use it."

"He did?" Legas remarked with a mischievous expression. "That sounds like a great story!" He turned to the Swordsman's father, who was grinning.

Over the Swordsman's protests, he began to speak. "We were up in the woods, on a hunting trip. Zander was about ten years old, I think. We had been traveling to one of our favorite places to hunt, and it was getting dark. It was also very cold, something Zander did not like at all. Unfortunately, we had forgotten flint for making a fire." He looked at Zander. "As I recall, it was Zander's responsibility to bring it."

The Swordsman visibly rolled his eyes and shook his head. His father ignored him and continued. "We gathered some kindling and a couple of small branches and tried to use a stick—the technique of twirling it to create enough friction to generate enough heat for the kindling to burn. By this time, Zander is shivering so hard, we can hear his teeth rattle." He winked at Zander's mother, patiently listening with her arms crossed. "Zander could be quite stubborn and had refused to pack the jacket his mother asked him to bring." The Swordsman's mother smiled at the memory.

"We couldn't get the kindling to light. Zander was getting very impatient."

"And very cold," the Swordsman interjected.

His father smiled and continued. "He grabbed the stick to try and twirl it himself, but to no avail. In frustration, he thrust out his hands toward the kindling and POOF! A lick of fire left his hands and lit the kindling."

Legas grinned at the Swordsman, who shifted uncomfortably in his chair. "Well, I had to start somewhere, didn't I?" he retorted.

"Indeed," Legas replied. He looked the huge man up and down. "I just never imagined you being so stubborn," he laughed. "I heard the story of how Rugal was able to do the Sepharim power transfer, and you destroyed two gormalins with your *dynamis.*"

"I couldn't have done it without Rugal's power transfer," the Swordsman admitted. "My *dynamis* is not that powerful on its own." He grinned. "But it still comes in handy if someone forgets the flint. And, of course, our basic techniques have served me well."

He turned to his father with a proud grin. "Remember when you were trying to teach me how to create a mental shield so that we could walk by unnoticed? After you were kidnapped, I used it to protect King Hamideh from a mother bear."

The Swordsman's father and mother smiled with pride at their son. "Well done, Zander," his father clapped him on the shoulder, then his expression grew serious. "Soldar must be being held at the castle. It will be difficult to rescue him." He leaned back and rubbed his chin, directing his gaze at Legas. "What exactly do you wish to map?"

"We want to map the forces that the Neliphim have at their disposal for the coming war. While the battle will be fought on the other side of the ocean, knowing the enemy's capabilities will provide important information."

"I can show you the shipyards," Kenrik spoke up. "The main fleet is kept on a stretch of beach near where I was assigned to work on building ships."

"That would be most useful," Legas nodded at the young man. "Perhaps it would be best to search out the land at night. It will be harder to see, but we'll be much less likely to get caught."

Finn's father spoke up. "The Neliphim reserve only a select few to learn the art of war through swordsmanship and archery. My work detail goes by their practice yards. I can provide information on them."

Legas nodded his appreciation and turned to the Swordsman. "Is that acceptable, Tamadar?" he asked formally.

The Swordsman looked at the small group seated about the hut's main living area and nodded. "It is a good plan, I think. You and Kenrik can work on mapping out the enemy's military capabilities." He scratched his head. "We still need to figure out how to rescue Soldar."

Finn's father glanced at the Swordsman's father, who nodded, then raised his hand to get the Swordsman's attention. "I think I might have an idea about that."

"Feelings are not always truth; they can be elusive and
unreliable."
~ Jackal, encouraging Rugal

"You are going to wear a path into the ground," Rugal
observed, watching Yandin pacing around the courtyard. "Take a breath and relax," he advised. "It's going
to be okay."

Yandin brushed his sandy hair back from his eyes and
wiped his palms on his tunic. "I'm just nervous, is all."

"Believe me, I understand," Rugal replied with a smile. "I
still get butterflies thinking about Lissa." He glanced at the
path leading to the castle. "Speaking of which, here she
comes."

Lissa walked toward them in a brightly colored gown,
with a spring in her step. Her light brown hair cascaded
about her shoulders, and her hazel eyes were shining with

excitement. She smiled at Rugal, then directed her gaze at Yandin. "Oh my, you look very handsome! Is that a new tunic?"

Yandin looked down, blushing. "Yes, Lissa. I hope Princess Gillian likes it."

Lissa reached out and patted the youth's arm. "She is certain to, I am sure!"

Smiling, Yandin looked up and a noise in the forest drew their attention. Yandin straightened up and pulled down on his tunic to adjust it. The three turned with big smiles to greet the princess. A horse came crashing through the trees, a bedraggled rider in the colors of Hamideh's castle guard barely holding on. The horse ran up to them and stopped. The rider slid to the ground and moaned, the broken shaft of an arrow protruding from his thigh. He looked up at the faces staring down at him with expressions of concern mixed with puzzlement.

"We were attacked on our way here. Princess Gillian has been kidnapped," he managed to gasp.

Yandin looked at the man in disbelief. Rugal, taking in the situation, grabbed the horse's reins. "Come on, Yandin. Help me lift him back onto the saddle. Be careful of that shaft. We need to get him back to the castle where we can remove it and bind his wounds."

Yandin and Rugal lifted the man back into his saddle while Lissa held his horse steady. They started to run back to the castle, but the man yelped in pain.

"Just walk him, Yandin," Rugal cautioned the youth. "Bouncing him at a trot is hurting him."

Yandid nodded and slowed his pace. Jackal and Mura were there to meet them at the castle entrance, having been watching out the window in hopes of glimpsing Princess Gillian's arrival.

"What happened?" Jackal asked as he helped the wounded man off his horse.

"I don't know," he gasped. "We were ambushed right after we had made our way through the mountains of central Elayas, while we were traversing the Great River—At the point where it would have brought us to the forests west of Cargoa and south of Laran."

He gazed at Jackal, and a look of distress crossed his face. "The other three guards were killed by arrows, coming out of nowhere. I was struck by this arrow and fell to the ground. Before I could do anything, Princess Gillian was swept from her horse by a warrior dressed in black, and the strangest thing I have ever seen happened. The warrior blew a whistle, and a huge sea creature erupted from the river. It looked like a dragon, except it had a snake-like body of thick coils and fins protruding from its cheeks. Princess Gillian's captor picked her up and placed her on a saddle that was strapped to the creature's back and mounted the saddle ahead of her."

"I would wager it was Krakos riding the leviathan, the same man that captured Soldar and shot an arrow at me," Rugal interjected, his eyes flashing at the memory.

"But why?!" Yandin gasped. "Why would anyone want Princess Gillian?" he choked out, holding back a sob.

"She is King Hamideh's sister," Jackal replied, as he continued to help the wounded guard, walking him through the castle entrance. "The enemy wants to use her as leverage against King Hamideh in the coming war." Spying Melad, he called out. "Get a doctor!"

The castle steward took one look at the situation and ran down the hallway.

"Come, you can rest in here," Jackal instructed, leading the guard into one of the rooms reserved for guests on the bottom floor. He laid him on the bed, and, noting the guard's anguish and sensing it had more to do with Gillian's kidnapping and less to do with the shaft sticking out of his thigh, he gripped the distraught man's hand.

"It will be okay," he soothed. "We will find her and get her back." His eyes turned steely. "I promise."

The doctor entered and immediately began examining where the arrow had entered the guard's thigh. An experienced physician, he quickly pulled out the arrow at the stem. The guard gasped, then passed out.

The doctor slathered some medicine onto the thigh area. "He's fortunate. The arrowhead didn't splinter. Plenty of rest, and he will be fine in a few days."

Jackal nodded and turned to Rugal. "It sounds like the Neliphim are taking Princess Gillian to their lands across the sea. For now, all we can do is trust that the Swordsman and his crew will find her."

Yandin's face crumpled in dismay. "I'll go rescue her!"

Rugal looked at the young man with sorrow in his eyes. "If we are going to have any hope of defeating the evil that is coming, we will need your blacksmith skills here." He reached out and squeezed Yandin's shoulder. "No one is more capable than the Swordsman. If anyone can find her and get her back, it is he."

"But how will he know she has been captured?" Yandin wiped his wet cheeks with the back of his hand.

"I don't know," Rugal admitted. "But he will find her, somehow."

"ARE you sure they should leave now?" Rugal asked almost plaintively.

Lissa and Mura were mounted on their horses, a contingent from the castle guard surrounding them. Mura's white mare danced in the early morning air. Lissa was riding a new horse, a gift from Johan and the Kargoliths. Her mare was a dappled grey with a finely shaped head. Much to Lissa's delight, the mare was exceptionally fleet of foot.

Jackal put his arm around Rugal. "It's the right thing to do, son. The Ring of Rosin said, 'end of winter.' Frakar has already sent men to kidnap our people twice. The weather is starting to warm. We must be ready." He rubbed his hand over his face. "The beacon fires will be critical for knowing when the Neliphim arrive on our shores and where to direct our troops. We must set the beacons up now."

Rugal straightened his shoulders, took a breath, and nodded. He walked over to Lissa's horse and began fussing with her stirrup. She looked down at him and smiled. "It will be okay, my love. And we will be in constant contact."

*I love you.*

Rugal smiled up at his beloved.

*I love you, too. Be careful!*

*I will.*

Mura glanced at Jackal, and he walked over and reached up for her hands. She leaned over for a kiss and they lingered a moment, gazing into each other's eyes.

"I like it better when we aren't separated," he said huskily.

"Me, too," Mura smiled down at him and stroked his cheek. "Hopefully, the day will come when it is no longer necessary to part."

Jackal nodded and squeezed her hands, then released them and stepped back. He turned to the guards. "Keep your charges safe."

"We will," the twelve men chorused. Mura and Lissa

turned their horses onto the path that led southward, with guards in front and in back.

Rugal and Jackal stood watching until they disappeared from view. Rugal rubbed his face and sighed, then looked at his father. "I guess we best get Tonar positioned as well."

Jackal gazed proudly at his son. Rugal was bearing the burden of kingship well. "Yes, that is a very good idea. The networks are still in place from our orchestrated attack on Oldag and his minions. I would suggest Tonar stay here in Cargoa. The Patriotes network is extensive. He can use Treble to bring messages to their leaders. Tonar has already heard from Johan and, if necessary, some Kargoliths will be available to send messages by horse."

"I have another idea about that, Father," Rugal replied. "Perhaps we can borrow some banyar birds and their handlers from the Arlesians. That would provide us a way to communicate across all of our forces. It would be invaluable." He waved his hands. "It might even be the difference between victory and defeat."

"That's a brilliant idea," Jackal paused. "But from what I have heard, they haven't been very cooperative. I know they have agreed to mobilize their ships, but only because one of their ships was recently attacked and destroyed by Frakar's leviathan."

"I know there is one thing King Nakasan wants." He sighed. "But Hamideh is not going to like it."

Jackal shot Rugal a knowing look. "Flash?"

Rugal nodded. He sighed again. "I would be devastated to lose Tag. I hate to ask him, but we haven't much time."

"It would certainly smooth the way," Jackal agreed. "And we need to be able to communicate. How are you going to ask him?"

Rugal thought for a moment. "Another letter, I suppose. Treble knows the way."

"Utilizing the banyars will be to his advantage, too," Jackal observed.

"I know," Rugal replied. "But Hamideh is very attached to Flash." His eyes grew moist. "There is something special about that big red horse." He shook himself and straightened his shoulders. "I'll write a message and ask Treble to deliver it. If he leaves this afternoon, we should have a response by tomorrow evening."

Jackal gazed at his son sympathetically. "Sometimes we have to make hard decisions."

"I never asked for any of this," Rugal suddenly choked out. "Sometimes I wish I was back at the Sepharim school learning how to control my *dynamis* under Felan's instruction. Those were much simpler days." He looked hesitantly at his father. "Sometimes I get my old feelings to run away."

Jackal stepped over and drew Rugal into a hug. "Believe me, we all feel that way sometimes. But it's how we respond to those feelings that count. Feelings are not always truth; they can be elusive and unreliable. We can recognize those negative thoughts as pesky and untrue." He stepped back and touched his son's cheek, wiping the tears streaking down it with his thumb. "You are strong and courageous, and you are not alone. We will fight together to safeguard our people."

Rugal wiped his face with his hand and nodded. "I best compose that letter to Hamideh. We will need to get everyone in place before the Neliphim invade."

"I find myself feeling a little lost without Mura. Let's get lunch, and I'll help," Jackal offered with a grin. Rugal smiled his agreement, and father and son headed back to the castle.

# SEVENTEEN

*Old memories influence new ones.*
~ Tolan Proverb

Soldar sat in a chair by the fire, staring into the flames. The nights were chilly, and being locked in the sparsely furnished room, he had little to occupy himself except for his thoughts. Still, he was grateful that Ferrous had seen fit to have him imprisoned in a guest room of the castle rather than a dungeon. He wrapped the blanket he had been using to help fight off the evening chill a little tighter and closed his eyes. Seeing Ferrous reminded him of his younger days, when he had first arrived at King Rosin's court. An image from the distant past welled up from his memory, and he allowed his thoughts to wander back in time.

"Soldar, there you are," Lindran, one of King Rosin's counselors, entered the library. "King Rosin is looking for you." He glanced at the books spread across the table and picked up one of the tomes, reading the letters on its spine. "The History of Tolan during King Hakarta's Reign." He glanced curiously at the young man sporting a brown beard and glasses. "Do you have a special interest in Tolan?"

"I have a special interest in everything," Soldar chuckled. "But since King Handerbin has only been on the Tolan throne a handful of years, I thought it might be helpful to understand his father's reign. Lady Mura is meeting with the Tolan diplomatic corps next week." He looked down and blushed. "I was hoping to accompany her. Perhaps I could be of service."

Lindran eyed Soldar thoughtfully. "You have the right spirit. An inquisitive mind and a penchant for history and government." He rubbed his chin thoughtfully. "You haven't been here long, but you have certainly been diligent. Keep doing what you are doing," he advised. "Your work is being noticed." He smiled at the young man. "You best leave your books—no one will bother them. You don't want to keep the king waiting."

Soldar nodded, jumping up and straightening his tunic. He followed the older man out of the library. They startled Ferrous rounding a corner on the way to King Rosin's personal quarters and his friend jerked back and gave him an inquisitive look. He shrugged his shoulders in return, hurrying to keep up with Lindran.

He would never forget the anxiety he felt, being called to come before the king. What could the king possibly want from him? He took a deep breath as the counselor knocked on the door.

"Come in."

Soldar slid by Lindran and into the room, where the king was seated in a chair, studying an object on a table in the sitting area of his room. He looked up and pointed at another chair. "Sit, please."

Soldar slipped into the chair King Rosin had indicated. He glanced sideways at the king, surprised at his casual dress. He had only seen Rosin in court, dressed in the protocol of his office as king. His brown hair, peppered with grey, gave him a natural dignity and kingly authority.

Rosin turned and looked at Soldar with a smile. "Thank you for coming. As our recently appointed scholar, I think this will be of interest to you."

Soldar hesitated, and Rosin reached over and squeezed his shoulder. "I know you aren't used to being at court, but I promise you, we are just regular people. The difference between me and any citizen of Elayas is that I have a responsibility to each citizen to defend and protect them." He gazed solemnly at Soldar. "And I need your help."

Soldar straightened in his chair and glanced curiously at the object on the table, then back at the king. "I will do anything I can to help!"

"Good man," the king shifted in his chair and picked up the simple but beautifully polished box that was on the table, the object of his study. Rosin reached down and opened the box to reveal its contents: a key made of gold. Soldar gasped as Rosin lifted it up, the emblem of the Sepharim and ancient script engraved along its length.

"What is it?" he whispered, sensing the key was part of something profound.

Rosin looked up. "You can never share what I am about to tell you, without permission of the reigning sovereign of Elayas. Can you make that promise?"

Soldar gulped and nodded.

"Good," Rosin picked up the key and lifted it for Soldar to examine.

"This key is called the Key of Power and has been held by the sovereigns of Elayas for centuries. It was first forged by a

Sepharim master. It has been imbued with the power to recognize the true king of Elayas, for it is only the king who can feel its power. The key can be used to focus and amplify the *dynamis* of the rightful king when it is in his proximity or on his person. It will allow the king to exert his *dynamis* for an extended period of time otherwise not possible."

Soldar reached out hesitantly, and Rosin dropped the key in his palm. He rubbed his finger along the script engraved along its side. "To live is to serve."

Rosin grinned at him. "You have studied well! Only a handful of people can read the ancient script. Well done!"

Soldar squirmed in his chair, blushing. "Thank you, Sire." He took a shaky breath. "But why am I here?"

"Great question," Rosin laughed. "Your curiosity will stand you well in your chosen profession." His tone turned serious. "You are here because the secret of the key must be safeguarded by a chosen few and passed down from generation to generation. You are here to become one of the Hashomer—Keeper of the Key."

Soldar's eyes widened, and he leaned back and stroked his beard as a thought occurred to him, "The tapestry in the great hall, the one of you holding the key in the air and battling the pirate ships."

"Yes?" Rosin tilted his head and raised an eyebrow.

"Something happened with the key." He paused, trying to recall the tapestry. "There is an array of mirrors. And lightning." He scratched his head. "The lightning was coming from the key, I think. It was striking the array of mirrors, which directed the lightning at the enemy ships." His eyebrows crinkled as he thought harder. "There are flames on the ships." He looked at Rosin. "The lightning came from the key, reflected off the mirrors, and set the ships on fire—but how?" He paused, thinking. "And we don't have an array of mirrors such as what is portrayed in the tapestry. At least, I have never seen one."

Rosin leaned forward and held out his hand. Soldar dropped the key in his palm. Rosin grasped the key and walked over to the wall. He ran his hand behind one of the wall sconces holding the candles that served to illuminate the room. He pushed down, and the sconce swung to the side. Soldar jumped back as a portion of the wall opened up, revealing a large, ornately carved wooden box on a shelf.

"You are correct, Soldar. We don't have the ability to make mirrors the size needed to do what I did that day. But someone else does. The same person who made the Key of Power possessed a very special *dynamis*." He walked over to the shelf and picked up the box. It was one and one-half times the length of a man's elbow to the tip of his hand and almost as tall. A metal plate with a hole was affixed to the front. Rosin brought the box to the table. He glanced at Soldar, then held up the key, positioned it into the hole, and turned it.

The lid to the box opened, and five mirrors rose from its depths, floating in the air above the box. Rosin gave the key a final turn, and the mirrors spread apart, growing in size. The sitting area became very crowded as each mirror increased to the size of a man. Rosin withdrew the key and, holding it in his hand, he focused his gaze on the mirrors. With a look of extreme concentration, he extended his *dynamis* and spread them out further, rotating them. He turned toward Soldar, who was standing pressed against the wall, eyes wide and mouth agape.

"The Key of Power is a conduit for the holder's *dynamis,* and it also activates the mirrors. You saw lightning in the tapestry. That is a picture of me channeling my *dynamis* through the key, to bounce off the mirrors and strike my target."

"But why do you need the mirrors?" questioned Soldar. "Why not aim your *dynamis* directly at your target?"

"I wish it was that easy," Rosin sighed. "The key is tremendous, but the mirrors are imbued with the ability to amplify my power even more. Without the mirrors, my *dynamis* through the key wouldn't have been hot enough to set the ships on fire. The mirrors are fixed to the key."

Soldar's eyebrows crinkled, and he tugged at his beard in thought. "I understand. The mirrors magnify the lightning and direct it to a focal point that becomes hot enough for combustion." He looked intently at Rosin. "Can anyone use the Key of Power to control the mirrors?"

"Only the person recognized by the key as the king of Elayas," Rosin responded. "But there is still great danger for its misuse." He blew out a breath and pinched his lips, then continued. "The fact that it is portable is a blessing and a curse. Just imagine the king falling into the hands of an enemy. He could be coerced into using the mirrors against his people, if the stakes were high enough. We must always safeguard against that possibility. That is why we must keep the location and the potential of the box of mirrors secret."

Rosin put the key back into the hole and turned it back to its original position. The mirrors shrank to their original size and floated back to the interior of the box. Rosin closed the lid with a firm snap and sighed. "It is unfortunate that I had to use the mirrors in front of witnesses when I was defending our shores from those marauders." He gazed intently at Soldar, who had relaxed and stepped to the table to examine the box more closely. "But no one fully understood what was happening. They didn't know the mirrors were unnatural." Rosin gave a short laugh. "Many people have gone looking for those mirrors, and the prevailing thought is that they were destroyed in a storm."

Soldar met his gaze. "How many people know about this?"

"Well," Rosin scratched his head. "Everyone knows that the Key of Power is a symbol of the king of Elayas, and that it can help him amplify and focus his *dynamis*. After Meron, the master tapestry maker, decided to do a tapestry of the battle for the great hall, I think many people wondered about the exact mechanism I used. But people who actually know the secret of the Key of Power and the mirrors are, let's see...My mentor in the Sepharim knew, for he was the one who passed it to me. But he is no longer of this world." He paused and looked at Soldar. "There's you. And there's me."

Soldar's head jerked up, and his eyes widened. "Only us?" he stammered.

"Yes," Rosin gazed sharply at Soldar. "It must stay that way. If it falls into the wrong hands, it could be used to destroy Elayas. We must keep the secret between me and you."

"But why tell me?" Soldar put his hand to his throat and looked at Rosin uncertainly.

"You are the king's scholar. As such, you are the repository of knowledge. Before you were brought into this role, I had you thoroughly investigated. I know you are a man of honor."

Soldar licked his lips and nodded. He straightened his shoulders. "Thank you, Sire. Your secret is safe with me."

Rosin looked at Soldar and grinned, then picked up the box and returned it to its shelf. He swung the sconce back into place. "Enough for one day. We don't want to arouse curiosity."

Soldar left the king's rooms and met Ferrous in the dining hall for dinner that evening as usual. "What was that all about?" Ferrous asked.

Soldar, remembering King Rosin's words, shook his head. "I don't know exactly. He wants me to catalog some artifacts for him, I think."

Ferrous nodded, his curiosity seemingly satisfied, and Soldar breathed a sigh of relief. He didn't want to break his promise, and Ferrous was his best and oldest friend.

The air became colder as the fire crackled, the wood almost completely burned. Soldar stirred out of his reverie and noticing the fire was nearly reduced to just embers, got up and added another log. Gazing into the fire, an unexpected tear rolled down his cheek. Stirring up old memories reminded him of how much they had lost when Oldag killed King Rosin and had taken over Elayas. His heart hurt for the friend he knew as Ferrous, but he felt a steely resolve against Frakar, the person he had become.

CHAPTER

# EIGHTEEN

*When a Leviathan cries, tears fall from the sky.*
~ Legend of the Sea

"Finn, this way," Kenrik hissed. "You will be out in the open if you continue down that path."

"Is there anyone guarding the ships?" Legas asked in a low voice, looking around.

"No," Kenrik replied. "No one should be about. I just don't want to invite trouble in case someone is out for a late-night stroll."

Moonlight brightened their surroundings, and the Swordsman, Legas, Kenrik, and Finn did their best to stay camouflaged in the sparse vegetation. Fields of timber rolled through the hills around the compound and castle, but as they neared the beach where the shipyards were located, it became harder to move stealthily through the brush terminating into the sandy beach. Kenrik pointed to an area where several large boulders were stacked on top and against each other. The three crouched and ran through the brush until they came up against the huge rocks and slid to the ground to catch their breath.

Kenrik peeked around the end boulder and pointed. "Krakos keeps the ships on this side. Each boat is either moored along the coastline or dragged up onto the beach." He pointed at the one closest to them. "See the hull with its overlapping planks? We learned from the Arlesian shipmaster that by cutting the timber that Finn's crew supplies along the grain instead of across it, the planks become more pliable. This allows the ships to ride rough waves. We also build internal ribs, knees, and thwarts to strengthen it. These ships can be sailed or rowed."

"It's a shame we don't have this expertise in Elayas," Legas observed. He tried to discern how many ships were on the beach. "It looks like there aren't that many," he commented hopefully.

"Unfortunately, the fleet is fairly large," Kenrik replied. "It consists of twenty boats capable of holding fifty people and seven boats capable of holding two hundred."

Legas did a quick calculation in his head. "So, we can expect an invading force of approximately twenty-four hundred." He gave a low whistle. "That is a large force to be reckoned with." He pulled a pad out of his pocket and made some notes.

Kenrik nodded, his face cloudy. "It looks like the majority of the fleet has already set sail. I'm sorry we have had a part in building it."

Finn choked back a sob. She looked at Legas with her eyes glistening. "It was easy to think of the trees as needing nurturing, like any living thing. We tried not to think about what their destiny was to be."

The Swordsman reached out and patted her back, and looked with compassion at Kenrik. "You did what you had to do. No one will blame you for it. And now you are coming to the aid of Elayas by gathering important information that will help us prepare." He paused and glanced at the boats that were left and then back to Kenrik. "I'm wondering, do you think we can sabotage any of them, without them knowing until they have already put to sea? We don't want to give our presence away, but whatever we can do to impede their progress would be beneficial to our cause."

Kenrik leaned back against the boulder and thought about the possibilities. He finally looked at the Swordsman and smiled. "We can tear holes in the sails. That won't be discovered until they unfurl them. First, they will row to get out of the harbor." He directed his gaze toward the boats. "They will be able to repair them, but it will slow them down."

"Excellent idea," Legas agreed. He reached into his boot and pulled out a long knife. He grinned at the Swordsman, Finn, and Kenrik, eyebrows raised. "Shall we?"

Kenrik smiled and led the way, running at a crouch down the beach. They reached one of the smaller schooners that had been dragged up the beach and climbed aboard. Kenrik located the mainsail where they could cause the most damage, and while Finn and Kenrik held the edges, Legas and the Swordsman artfully cut gashes into the fabric so that they would not be easily noticed. The band of saboteurs were on their fourth vessel, this one floating in the harbor close to the shore, when they heard crashing waves.

The sea had been calm up to that point, and Finn ran crouching to the side of the hull and peeked over it to see what was happening.

"It's the sea creature!" she gasped.

The others came up beside her to see for themselves. The

leviathan swam up to the beach and lowered its head to the sand, half in and half out of the water. Two people climbed out of the saddle attached to the sea creature's back and dropped to the ground. The leviathan looked plaintively at one of the figures and cried, blue streams coming out of its eyes. The man shook his head. He brought a whistle to his lips and blew it, gesturing for the leviathan to return to the sea, the saddle still attached to its neck. The creature dove into the water and swam swiftly, disappearing into the murky depths.

The Swordsman, Legas, Kenrik, and Finn ducked down, watching from the boat. The Swordsman gripped his sword, and Legas held his long knife at the ready. Finn and Kenrik stiffened as they watched the two figures walking toward them.

"It's Krakos!" Finn whispered urgently. "Frakar's second in command."

The Swordsman observed the bow slung on Krakos' back along with a quiver of arrows. "He must be the one Rugal told us about, the one who shot a magic arrow at him when he and Johan were at the river."

Kenrik nodded. "Yes, Krakos is the one that rides the leviathan. Frakar controls the creature with his mind, and Krakos carries out Frakar's orders, using the whistle Frakar gave him to communicate with it."

"Soldar was kidnapped by Krakos and the leviathan. It seems they have another victim," the Swordsman observed. As the figures came closer, the Swordsman's pulse quickened. He peered through the darkness to be sure. "It's Princess Gillian!" he whispered, his voice filled with anger. "Krakos kidnapped Prince Hamideh's younger sister, Princess Gillian!"

"But why?" Finn asked, puzzled. "What good would that do?"

The Swordsman's voice shook with fury. "Frakar knows

that Tolan is joining Elayas in our effort to defend our lands from the Neliphim invasion. By kidnapping Princess Gillian, Frakar has some leverage against Tolan. King Hamideh will not want to see his sister harmed."

Krakos held Princess Gillian's arm loosely as they passed the group hiding in the boat. Both were soaking wet from their recent ride across the ocean. Gillian walked tight-lipped, unwillingly matching Krakos' stride.

"He must be taking her to the castle," Legas whispered. "Frakar will want to glean any information from her that he can."

The thought of Frakar interrogating Hamideh's younger sister was unbearable. At Legas' words, the Swordsman stood up and, with a roar, jumped out of the boat and ran toward the two figures walking up the beach, sword in hand. Krakos spun around. Seeing the huge man bearing down on him, he shoved the princess onto the sand and drew an arrow out of his quiver, intent on bringing his bow up to shoot the oncoming threat.

The Swordsman pumped his legs even harder, barreling toward the evil warrior in an attempt to get to him before he could loose an arrow from his bow. Krakos nocked his arrow and planted his feet, taking aim at the huge man just a few yards away. He pulled back and released the arrow, which soared through the air. The Swordsman tried to leap out of the way of its trajectory, but the arrow flew into his thigh. The Swordsman bellowed as it struck him, then literally froze as his body turned into ice.

"You are fortunate I didn't have time to pick my arrow," Krakos said. "That one will only keep you frozen. You would have found the fire arrow most unpleasant."

He turned to Princess Gillian, standing a few feet away with a horrified expression. "Wait here, or I will try a different arrow on your would-be rescuer." He looked in the direction the Swordsman had appeared from and started walking toward the boat where the rest of the group was hiding. He walked up to the hull and peered inside. Legas and Kenrik, seeing no way to hide, reluctantly stood up.

"Who are you, and what are you doing here?" Krakos demanded.

Kenrik spoke up. "I'm a shipbuilder. I was just showing my friends the ship I have been working on."

"If that's true, why did that huge man attack me?"

Kenrik shrugged. "I can't answer that. Me and my friend," he indicated Legas, "we were just enjoying the night air."

"Nice try, Kenrik," Krakos smiled grimly. "I know who you are, and that you are outside of your compound. You've been missing for several weeks and now you show up with two strangers." He gestured curtly for them to get out of the boat. "You can drag your frozen friend with you. I am certain Frakar will want to have a conversation with all of you. Bring him to the castle," he ordered brusquely. "You know the way."

He turned on his heel and started moving up the beach to where Princess Gillian waited, next to the frozen man holding his sword. She turned to Krakos with tears in her eyes. "You can't leave the Swordsman like this!"

He grabbed her arm again. "Come, they will follow and bring your frozen friend."

Legas clambered down the schooner and onto the beach. Kenrik, leg flung over the hull, looked back inside the schooner, and Finn appeared. Her red hair fell about her shoulders, and in the moonlight, she looked more beautiful than he had ever seen her. She put her finger to her lips and met his gaze with a determined look on her face. He nodded, then jumped to the sand and jogged to catch up with Legas, careful not to arouse any suspicion about Finn's presence.

Legas and Kenrik walked up to where the Swordsman

stood frozen. Kenrik pointed to a wagon with two wheels and two poles a man could grasp for moving objects, used to bring planks of timber down the beach to the ships being built.

"We can use that."

He ran to the wagon and, moving between the poles, grasped each one and started walking toward the Swordsman. Bringing it alongside the huge frozen man, he and Legas managed to slide the Swordsman into the bed of the wagon, being careful not to disturb the arrow for fear of harming the Swordsman further. They worked together, each pulling a pole of the wagon as they walked up the sandy beach in the direction of the castle.

"Why didn't Krakos stay to force us to do his bidding?" Legas asked, as they pulled the wagon up the beach. "How did he know we would comply?"

"He knows we have nowhere else to go," Kenrik replied. "And if we hope to release the Swordsman from his frozen state and rescue the princess, we must follow him." He lowered his voice, even though Krakos and the princess were out of sight. "Finn will surely come up with something. She is very resourceful."

# CHAPTER
# NINETEEN

"Sometimes our mental battles are bigger than our physical
ones."
~ King Johan of Kargolith

"Over there," Lissa swept her hair out of her eyes. The wind was gusting on the beach of Elayas's southern shore. "I think we should build the shelter there," she pointed at a hill that topped the section of beach.

Mura followed the direction Lissa was pointing. "Yes. That seems as good a place as any," she agreed. She gestured to the guards, and they moved in closer so they could hear her above the wind.

"Betzar, could you please ask your men to build a wind-break there?" Mura indicated the section Lissa had pointed out. "It will need to be sufficient for a signal fire to be built successfully. I think it should be more substantial than the ones your men built during our journey here. Now that we are on the coast, the wind will be stronger."

"Yes, Lady Mura," the strong, burly guard dipped his head in agreement. He moved to direct his men while Lissa and Mura scouted the area for sufficient brush to fuel the fire.

"I think we are in a good place, south of Cargoa to the shoreline," Mura commented as they worked. "But we will need coverage both east and west along the southern coast as well as the eastern coast of Elayas, since we don't know where the Neliphim will make landfall. I think we should each lead a party. You can go east, and I'll go west. We can travel along the coastline to place the beacons and meet up where the Selba River feeds into the Great River when we're done. Could you please inform Rugal?"

At the mention of Rugal, Lissa smiled, and color rushed to her cheeks. She nodded and looked off into the distance.

*We are at the coast, dearest.*

*So nice to hear your voice! Are you okay?*

*We are doing well. The guardsmen have done a thorough job preparing the beacons and building windbreaks around them during our journey southward, each one a half day's journey apart. We have also recruited local Patriotes to man them. We must address the coastlines now. We need to have beacons going both east and west, at least two days ride each. I will direct six guardsmen, and we will go three days east, building seven beacons evenly spaced. Mura is also going to direct six guardsmen going two days west and building five beacons evenly spaced. That should be suffi-cient. We will then travel northward and meet at the junction of the Selba River and the Great River and return together.*

*That sounds like a good plan. I'll inform Jackal. Be careful, my love.*

*Always. I miss you.*

*I miss you, too.*

Lissa shook herself and returned her gaze to Mura, "We are all set."

"Hold your arm higher!" The tall, lithe man in a blue tunic with a braid on the shoulder indicating he was part of the Arlesian Communications Corps instructed Yandin. They stood in the courtyard and gazed skyward. "You need to have it high enough that the banyar sees the flag and recognizes you are his receiver, yet level enough that he can land gracefully."

Yandin nodded, adjusting his arm in accordance with the Arlesian's instructions. Rugal thought putting Yandin in charge of the banyar contingent for the castle made sense in more ways than one. Yandin had a natural affinity for animals, well-shown in how he handled the royal horses, and it would be a welcome distraction from Princess Gillian's kidnapping.

The bird that had been a tiny mote in the sky descended, its wings pumping as it braked and prepared for its landing. Approaching Yandin, it put forth its clawed feet and back-winged, landing gracefully on Yandin's outstretched arm. It gazed inquisitively into Yandin's face and held out its leg. A piece of paper was strapped to it, which Yandin carefully removed with his other hand and tucked into a pocket of his tunic.

"Now feed him," instructed the Arlesian. "This is a critical part of his training. He must know that by coming here, he will be fed and watered and have a place to rest. In this way, we can expand his homing instinct to include the castle. You can feed him the food from your hand, then place him in the banyar house we constructed. By doing this, he will know that this place is a good place for him, and he will return here when he is released."

"Can that be done anywhere?" Yandin asked while feeding the banyar, the bird eagerly eating out of his hand.

"Indeed," the Arlesian replied. "We have sent members of my corps with banyars across the continent. King Hamideh of Tolan, King Johan of Kargolith, King Nakasan of Arlesia, and, of course, King Rugal will be able to communicate via the banyar network we are building."

"Is it true King Hamideh traded Flash for the banyar network?" Yandin asked.

"Rumor has it, King Nakasan is in possession of a magnificent red horse, a gift from the King of Tolan. I am not privy to the details."

Yandin nodded, gently stroking the banyar's feathers. The bird preened at his attention, and the Arlesian smiled. "Good work. I think this bird is imprinting nicely to the castle. Now, let's introduce him to his new home so he can finish eating, get something to drink, and rest. We will practice again tomorrow."

Yandin followed the Arlesian to the corner of the courtyard that housed the banyar's new living quarters, built to the Arlesian's specifications. The bird hopped off of his shoulder, flew to the little wooden structure, and disappeared inside.

ROHAN LEANED over Jakash's neck at a full gallop, coming out of the woods and reining him alongside Johan, who looked up from the leather bridle he was mending, startled at the horse's sudden appearance. Rohan jumped off his paint horse, landing almost on top of Johan, grabbing his twin and laughing. Both fell in the dirt and rolled as the other Kargoliths looked on, grinning at the two brothers. Johan may be king, but the Kargoliths were a spirited people who were not overly concerned with formality. They appreciated seeing the rough-and-tumble affection of their king and his younger brother. Jakash came to a halt and shook his body, blowing noisily, then turned around and nosed Rohan, who lay with his chest heaving with laughter on the ground. Johan jumped up first and held his hand out to his twin, who grasped it and drew him in for a back-pounding hug.

Johan stepped back and looked his brother up and down. "You are well, then," he grinned.

"Yes, brother," Rohan returned, grinning back. He turned toward the woods and gestured. "I have brought a friend from the Sepharim school."

Elgibran emerged from the woods, riding a bay gelding. He walked his horse up to Johan and Rohan and dismounted, smiling hesitantly.

Rohan turned to Johan. "Elgibran is my classmate. He helped me learn how to control my *dynamis*. He also has a deep appreciation for fine horses, and when I told him I was going home for a visit, he asked if he could come along and meet Raksh." Rohan grinned. "Apparently, your dun steed has become famous throughout the continent, thanks to carrying you on your exploits."

"Yes," Elgibran spoke up. "Kargoliths are renowned in Elayas for their horses and horsemanship."

Johan looked at the tall, skinny youth curiously, but custom dictated that he welcome his brother's friend first. "Come, you both must be hungry. We can converse over a meal."

The three young men sat cross-legged around a fire in front

of Johan's tent. "You haven't built a castle yet, brother?" Rohan teased, grinning mischievously.

Johan just shook his head and took another bite of bread and meat. Finishing it, he turned his attention to Rohan's friend and raised his eyebrows. "So, you want to meet Raksh? Why?"

Elgibran met Johan's gaze and nodded. "Yes, I am from Dalben. Our community is known for its dedication to horsemanship and fine horses. Raksh, the mighty dun ridden by the king of the Kargoliths, is known as an exceptional mount, smart, athletic, and loyal. The story of how he alerted King Rugal that you were in danger and that he found you after Rugal rescued you is frequently told at our gatherings. Raksh has become the standard by which other horses are judged. I wished to meet Raksh, and Rohan offered to bring me with him so I could."

Johan took a sip of ale. "What is your *dynamis*?" he asked, changing the subject.

Elgibran looked at Rohan, who nodded at his friend. Elgibran turned back to Johan. "I am able to transport objects through the air." He looked down and mumbled, "Although I am not very good at it."

Johan gave a low whistle. "A useful *dynamis* indeed." He returned his gaze to the fire and considered how to respond. "Finish up your meal." He winked at Rohan and smiled, then turned to Elgibran. "I'll let you take Raksh for a ride."

CHAPTER

# TWENTY

"Adversity has a way of bringing people together."
~ Jackal, commenting on the Patriotes and the Arlesians

"Any ideas?" Legas spoke in a low voice. They sat in chairs in the room Krakos had shoved them in after they had arrived at the castle with the Swordsman in tow.

Kenrik glanced at the Swordsman, still in a frozen state against the wall. He shook his head. "Not yet. The castle is impregnable, but Finn will figure out something." He gave a small smile. "She is very smart."

"That's good to know, but right now, we need to do something to release the Swordsman from the arrow's magic." Legas scratched his head. "I wonder if removing the arrow will remove the hold it has over the Swordsman."

He walked over to the Swordsman and examined the arrow sticking out of his thigh. Coming to a decision, he reached toward the embedded end, grabbed a hold of the arrow, and gave a quick jerk. The arrow came out of his thigh, leaving a hole where the point had entered. The Swordsman unfroze, the ice vanishing. Blood began to flow from the hole in his thigh. He moaned and slid to the ground, passing out.

Tearing off the sleeve of his tunic, Legas knelt beside the Swordsman and used it to press on the wound, staunching the flow of blood. He looked up at Kenrik, who stood helplessly watching. "The flow of blood is stopping. I think he fainted from the trauma he experienced. Let's see if we can wake him up."

Kenrik looked around the room, hoping to find something that would help the huge man who had risked his life in his attempt to rescue the princess. The room was bare except for the chairs. It was obvious Finn adored her uncle. They had to do something to help him, preferably before Krakos or Frakar showed up.

"I don't see anything," Kenrik's jaw clenched with frustration.

"It's okay," Legas replied in a soothing voice. "I'll use a Sepharim technique to wake him. Here, take my place and keep applying pressure."

Kenrik squatted next to the Swordsman, pressing down on the wound with Legas' impromptu bandage. Legas moved over by the Swordsman's head and placed his hands on either temple. He whispered some words in the ancient language, gently rotating his fingers in a circular motion. After a few moments, the Swordsman stirred and opened his eyes. "Legas," he managed to say. "Thank you."

Legas dropped his hands away from the Swordsman's head as the big man lifted it. Kenrik looked carefully under the cloth he had been pressing and gave a sigh of relief. "The bleeding has stopped." He left the bandage on top of the wound and held it loosely in place while the Swordsman managed to sit up and look around. "Where are we?"

"We are in Frakar's castle," Kenrik spoke up. "Krakos dumped us in this room when we arrived at the castle gates." He rubbed his cheek tiredly. "I'm not sure where he is keeping Princess Gillian, but she must be in the castle somewhere."

"And what of Finn?" the Swordsman asked, concern in his voice.

"She used her *dynamis* and remained undiscovered when Krakos found us in the hull of the ship," Kenrik replied. "Knowing Finn, she is somewhere about, but at least she remains undetected."

"Good girl," the Swordsman breathed. "She is clever like her mother." He looked at both men and sighed. "Unfortunately, between Princess Gillian, Soldar, and us, Frakar believes he has leverage. We have to escape so that Rugal and Hamideh won't be placed in an untenable position."

He paused in thought, eyebrows furrowed. "Our options are very limited."

"Remember, Finn's father had a plan for Soldar's rescue," commented Legas. "Finn is probably on her way to get his help." He gazed at Kenrik. "Your people have been very resilient and resourceful. What do you think they will do?"

"They will come for us, of that I have no doubt. But Krakos is Frakar's watchdog, and he is without conscience. They will be putting their lives in danger to rescue us."

"I think we should position the Tolan archers here," Jackal pointed at the large river running through the center of Elayas, often referred to by locals as the Great River because of its width and depth. "The Neliphim have boats that can travel up the river. We need to be ready to stop them." Rugal and Jackal were in the library, pouring over the map that Legas had created.

Rugal leaned over and studied the area that Jackal indicated. He stroked his chin, thinking. "If we don't have a force ready along its banks, we will be vulnerable. Would they be stationed on both sides?"

"They would have to be," Jackal studied the map further. "Unless we can force them to one side."

"Maybe that is where Argothal could be of help." He looked up at Jackal. "He did a great job herding the enemy when we overthrew Oldag, and again when we were confronting the Kargoliths."

Jackal grinned at his son. "Good thinking!" He paused. "But he may not be back from transporting the Swordsman from the Neliphim lands in time. We should alert Johan to send a force of Kargoliths to the west side of the Great River as well." He stood back and crossed his arms, gazing at the map, looking for vulnerable points. He pointed to the southern beaches. "This is a possible place for them to land, coming across the sea. And here," he pointed to the eastern coastline.

"We can position the rest of the Kargoliths and the Sepharim along the southern coast. The Kargoliths are the most mobile being on horseback and so can reposition themselves if needed elsewhere. Janar and Ethiod will be leading the Sepharim, and they can reinforce the Kargoliths with their *dynamis* as needed. The Kargoliths and Sepharim should complement each other well in their capabilities."

"Which leaves the Patriotes and the Arlesian fleet to defend the eastern coast. That sounds good. The Arlesians have been reluctant to join forces. They will be most effective if they are defending their own shores." Rugal paused, thinking. "That actually works better. Hamideh mentioned the Arlesians are unfamiliar with *dynamis* and wary of it, so asking the Patriotes to fight with the Arlesians makes better sense."

"Good point. We all have a role to play according to our gifts, *dynamis* or otherwise. And the Patriotes may just show them a thing or two. Adversity has a way of bringing people together." Jackal stretched. "It will also be advantageous to track their locations with the help of the Ring of Rosin," he gestured toward the map in front of them.

Melad entered the library, concern written on his face. "Excuse me, Sire, Jackal, I have a matter of some urgency. A note was received by King Hamideh when Frakar kidnapped Princess Gillian. Hamideh used a banyar bird to relay the message to you."

Rugal held out his hand, and Melad dropped a small scroll into it. "Thank you, Melad. Is the bird still here?"

"Yes, Sire. The training is proving very effective. It is eating now and will bed down for the night in the structure we have provided for it."

"Very good, Melad. I have a feeling I will be sending Hamideh a message in the morning."

"Yes, Sire." The head steward bowed briefly, and, stepping into the hallway, he closed the doors to the library.

Rugal unrolled the note with trembling hands, fearing the worst. Jackal walked over and read the scroll at the same time over Rugal's shoulder. Both men let out a breath of frustration.

*King Hamideh of Tolan, in reading this note, you now know I have kidnapped Princess Gillian, and I am holding her at my castle across the sea. My demand is simple. If you wish to see her again, you will step away from the coming conflict. Your Tolan archers are renowned. You will order them to disband and not participate in the coming war. I will hold her here until my victory is assured.*

A second piece of paper behind the first was from Hamideh, and Rugal held it so Jackal could read it, too.

*You know I can't let Gillian be harmed. I'm sorry.*

"Hamideh is in an impossible situation," Rugal muttered. He turned and looked at Jackal. "We can't allow Frakar to harm Gillian."

"I know, son," Jackal walked over and put his arm around Rugal. "We need to trust that what we do have, will be enough." He squeezed his shoulders. "It's not over yet."

# TWENTY-ONE

*Get help when you can, give help when you can.*
~ Kargolith Proverb

*Rugal! Can you hear me?! Wake up!*

Rugal jerked awake from a sound sleep.

"What?!" he spoke out loud, trying to orient himself.

He sat up in his bed and looked around. Moonlight peeked through the shutters of the window, kept closed against the chill of the night.

*It's me, dearest. Are you sleeping?*

*Not anymore,* Rugal tried to keep the annoyance out of his mental voice. A good night's sleep was hard to come by lately, but obviously Lissa had something important to share. *Are you okay?* He took a deep breath and slowly released it, composing himself.

*Yes, we are all doing fine. We are traveling along the eastern coast, setting up the signal beacons. It's just that something happened this evening when we paused to eat. Something I think you would want to know.*

Rubbing his eyes, Rugal swung his feet over the side of the bed.

*What happened, my love?*

*Well,...you remember you had an unusual dream about a giant sea creature a few days ago?*

*Of course.*

*I have met her mate! I was sitting on a log near the shoreline when a giant sea creature surfaced in front of me. It turned its eye to gaze upon me and asked what we were doing. I can communicate with the sea creature just like I can talk to Argothal!*

Rugal sat still for a few moments, absorbing Lissa's admission and what it might mean.

*What did he say?*

*He said he lives in the waters off of the coast of the Neliphim's lands. The sea creature Frakar has entrapped is his mate. They are leviathans.*

*Why doesn't Frakar entrap him as well?*

*I asked him that. He said Frakar's dynamis isn't strong enough to hold them both.*

*If his mate is across the sea, what is he doing here?*

Lissa's mental voice became tinged with excitement. *He wants to help us defeat Frakar, so he can rescue his mate, and they can return to their home under the sea.*

*Did he say how?*

He could visualize Lissa shaking her head, her light brown hair flowing with the motion.

*He's not sure. He can't do anything to harm his mate, of course, but perhaps he can help when the enemy ships arrive. In any case, he wants you to know that his mate is being held against her will. She did not want to transport anyone from Elayas across the sea without their consent. She also did not want to destroy the Arlesian ship. Frakar gave her no choice. The evil Krakos controls her with the whistle Frakar gave him.*

*Please tell him I know,* Rugal replied. *I know the sorrow it is causing her to have to do the things she is doing. I also know she saved Kenrik's life. Sigh... If we can overcome the Neliphim, maybe we can make things right for them when this is all over.*

*I will tell him, dearest. If you need his help, reach out to me, and I will let him know what you need.* Lissa paused a moment, her attention diverted. *I must go. We are finishing the final beacon placement.*

*Before you go, I have some disturbing news.* Even Rugal's mental tone sounded sad. *Princess Gillian has been kidnapped, much the same way Soldar was. She has been taken across the sea and is being held in Frakar's castle. Her ransom is for Tolan to not participate in the upcoming war.*

*Oh, no! What are you going to do?*

Rugal could hear the anguish in Lissa's voice. He focused on making his own voice as soothing as possible.

*Nothing. We can't risk Gillian. We will continue the fight without Tolan.*

*Oh my, how can we fight...but that's what we must...* Lissa stuttered as she tried to make sense of what happened to Princess Gillian and the impact of losing Tolan in their fight. *What about the Swordsman and his spy mission?*

*They have not returned. We don't know if they have run into any problems. I am worried that if Frakar was brazen enough to capture Gillian, then the Swordsman's mission may be compromised.* He tried to sound encouraging. *It will be okay. Stay safe, my love. Now, go do what you must, just as we all will.*

Rugal felt the emptiness he had always come to feel when their contact was broken. He laid down and tried to will himself to sleep, but thoughts of Lissa, the leviathans, Princess

Gillian, and Soldar all jumbled around his mind. Finally, he dozed into a fitful slumber.

Finn's father and the Swordsman's parents sat restlessly in their hut, awaiting everyone's return. Dawn broke across the eastern sky, and golden streaks of sunlight shone through the windows.

"Something must have happened," Finn's father paced the length of the hut. "Surely they would have returned here under the cover of night."

"Agreed," the Swordsman's father nodded. "We must do something, but what?"

Before anyone could answer, there was a quick knock on the door. Finn's father jumped up to open it, and Finn flew into his arms. He gave her a hug and then held her at arm's length, noting her tear-stained face. "What happened?"

Finn looked down, clenching her jaw and fists as she got the words out. "We were on the beach, sabotaging some of the boats, when Krakos appeared on the leviathan. He has kidnapped Princess Hamideh's younger sister, Princess Gillian, and was escorting her up the beach. When Uncle Zander saw him, he jumped out of the boat to attack him and save Gillian. Krakos froze Uncle Zander with one of his arrows and found Legas and Kenrik. He forced them to carry Uncle Zander in one of the work carts, and they all disappeared into Frakar's castle. I escaped using my *dynamis*. He didn't see me." Finn started to tremble, and her father lowered her into a chair. "We have to get them back!"

The Swordsman's mother wrapped her arms around Finn's shoulders and kissed the top of her granddaughter's head.

"Your Bappa is very clever, Finn. I am sure he and your father will be able to rescue all of them."

"Yes, we will," soothed her father. "We can use the plan I suggested to the Swordsman. We will have to expand on it since we now have four to rescue rather than one, but I think we can still do it. That is," he turned to the Swordsman's father. "If you are still willing."

He scratched his head. "I haven't used my *dynamis* in years. I may be a bit rusty, but I am willing to try."

Finn's father nodded. "Good. We'll have to wait until nightfall. If you can get Finn inside the castle, she knows the layout, and we can rescue the others."

"So, now that you have more hostages," Soldar gazed at Ferrous, who sat in one of the chairs in Soldar's room. Soldar was not surprised that the Swordsman had attempted to rescue him, but he was greatly disturbed at Ferrous' admission that not only had he captured Legas and Kenrik, he was also holding Princess Gillian hostage. He stared at the man that used to be his best friend. "What are you going to do with us?"

"Well, really, that's not up to me," Ferrous replied, taking a swig of ale. He had taken to visiting Soldar during the evening mealtime and had dinner brought to Soldar's room. He met Soldar's stare with lifeless eyes and sighed. "If you would reveal the secret of the key, we could partner together. I would give you Elayas to rule. You could prevent a lot of carnage. The Neliphim have already launched most of their ships. Krakos has his magic arrows. I believe Hamideh won't be participating now that I have his precious Gillian. Why, we even have the famous Swordsman captured," he chuckled. He sat up, and his eyes took on an eerie gleam. "Join me, old friend. It's a simple request, really. What's the secret of the Key of Power?"

Soldar leaned back and sighed, wiping his mouth with a napkin. "I can't."

Ferrous glared across the table at the rumpled scholar, eyes flashing. "Then I will have to capture Rugal and get the secret from him."

Soldar pinched his lips together and shook his head, "That won't work either."

Ferrous raised his eyebrows. "Why not?"

"I never had a chance to tell him. I meant to do so, but I have been away working with Ethiod on setting up schools across Elayas."

Ferrous' eyes narrowed, and he studied Soldar, who did his best to look nonchalant.

"Why are you telling me this now?"

"That's easy," Soldar replied. "As you already know, only the king of Elayas has the ability to wield the Key of Power. No need to capture Rugal to implement something he has no knowledge about." He looked at Ferrous with entreaty. "You have nothing to fear from them. I will withhold the information from Rugal as well if you promise not to attack. You can keep your lands here without fear of being taken over by Rugal."

"The only problem with your offer is that was never my fear. I will take over all of Elayas, and the entire continent, with or without the Key of Power," Ferrous replied. "But you will do better to tell me its secret."

"Ferrous," he leaned forward and allowed a note of entreaty to enter his voice. "Stop this. You have no family or friends here. All you have is forces bent on evil. Walk away. Make a different choice."

"I could never attain in Elayas what I have here," Ferrous replied, shaking his head.

"What does it gain you, if you lose your soul?" Soldar pleaded. "The Ferrous I knew would never do this."

"The Ferrous you knew doesn't exist anymore." Ferrous stood up abruptly. "Enough. The majority of my fleet should already be approaching Elayas. I have not done anything yet for the sake of our old friendship. But don't think that I won't for much longer." He walked past Soldar, opened the door and walked out. Soldar could hear the door's lock click behind him.

# TWENTY-TWO

"Need drives creative thinking."
~ Vanjarli, Master of the Sepharim, teaching his students how
to use their *dynamis*

The courier came riding at full gallop into the courtyard and up to the castle doors, shouting, "The beacon fire has been lit in position 4 of the southern shore!"

Rugal and Jackal came running out of the castle entrance, followed by Yandin, Melad, and the castle staff. The courier's horse lowered its head, its body dripping with sweat and breathing heavily. The courier dismounted, and Farin ran up, grabbed the reins, and walked the horse toward the stables to care for him. The courier turned to Rugal and sketched a quick bow. "Sire! The enemy has landed where the Great River pours into the Argonean Sea!"

"Have you any idea of the numbers?" Rugal asked.

"No," the courier frowned. "There's no way to tell. The beacon only alerts us that an enemy force has been sighted."

"That makes sense." Rugal nodded and gave the courier's shoulder a brief squeeze. "What is your name?"

"My name is Tilak."

"Well done, Tilak. Farin is taking care of your horse. You must be hungry and exhausted." He turned to Melad. "Please see to it that Tilak is fed a hearty meal and given a bed."

"Of course, Sire. Please follow me," Melad motioned to the young man. He gestured to his staff and Rugal and Jackal watched the crowd disperse to resume their duties, anxiety evident in their voices as they shared their responses to the news of the invasion with each other.

Rugal looked at Jackal and balled his fists, his eyes flashing and his jaw clenched. "It has begun."

Jackal returned his gaze. "Yes. Let's check the map and see where our troops are located in relation to the beacon at position 4."

Rugal followed Jackal into the library, and they both bent over the map that was spread across the large table in the center of the room. Rugal brought his hand wearing the Ring of Rosin to bear, placing it on one corner. The map illuminated, showing tiny figures on foot and horseback. Some of the figures had a bluish outline, indicating they were members of the Sepharim.

Jackal peered eagerly at the coastline, then blew out a breath of disappointment. "Just as I expected, although I hoped otherwise. We can only see our troops with Legas's *dynamis*, not the enemy's."

Rugal's eyebrows knit together. "Why do you think that is?"

Jackal frowned. "The Neliphim aren't human. They are forces of evil. They don't register on the map because they don't have souls." He met Rugal's eyes and sighed. "It looks like the Sepharim are stationed on the southern coast and the Kargoliths have split themselves between the west side of the Great River and the southern coast. I hope they are enough. Losing the Tolan archers has weakened our positions significantly."

"Shouldn't I head for the coast?" Rugal asked. "Now that we know where the enemy has landed, I should be leading our troops."

Jackal shook his head. "I know you are eager to defend Elayas, Sire, but for the moment, you can best serve here at the castle. It is early yet, and we don't know where all of the threats will be coming from." He eyed his son compassionately. "I know it's hard to wait, but it's not yet time."

Rugal bit his lip and nodded, then returned his attention back to the map. "What should we do next?"

"If the enemy forces are landing here, they are very close to where the Great River empties into the sea. I was afraid of that." Jackal pointed at the enemy's landing site, then ran his finger up the Great River. "They may split their forces and try to engage our coastal forces while others come up the Great River to reach our interior. They may even attempt to take Cargoa if they are able to traverse the Great River far enough north."

He indicated on the map where a band of Kargoliths were camped not too far west of the Great River. "Johan's men will have to meet the enemy at the junction of the Great River and Kalbin. If the Neliphim reach there and get past our forces, the city of Cargoa will be in harm's way."

"I think we should..." before Rugal could finish his

sentence, the door to the library flung open, and a courier ran inside. "Sire!" The youth gasped, breathing hard. "Beacon 11E reports that the enemy made landfall at their position on the eastern coast!"

Rugal and Jackal looked at each other, then at the map. The Arlesian ships and Patriotes were positioned north of their landing. The map showed their movement as they responded to the beacon, but it was impossible to tell if they would be able to contain the enemy. If the Neliphim breached their shores from the east, and the Great River from the west, they would be trapped, and the castle would be in danger.

*Lissa, can you hear me? Are you okay?*

Lissa smiled to herself. They were getting better at communicating. She could hear Rugal more easily when he reached out.

*Yes, dearest, I am here.*

*Where is here?* She could hear the anxiety in his mental voice.

All of the beacons have been placed, and we just met back up with Mura and her troops. We all arrived at the junction of the Great River and the Selba River this morning.

*Beacon 4 and Beacon 11E have been lit. The Neliphim are here.*

Lissa paused, processing Rugal's words. They had been working so hard to put the beacons in place in preparation that she had shoved any thought of the coming invasion to the back of her mind. She no longer had that option. She took a breath to compose herself.

*Lissa?*

*I'm here, Rugal. I was just absorbing the news. How can we help?*

Rugal glanced at Jackal, a question in his eyes. Jackal nodded in return.

*We think it best for you to remain where you are at. You are not in any immediate danger, and we need to know what the Neliphim are going to do. We can't see enemy troops on Legas' map, only our own. If you and Mura and your guardsmen can keep watch for enemy troops, that will help us position the Kargoliths that are upriver from you.*

*Of course, dearest. I will let Mura know.*

Rugal blew out a breath. *We hate to ask you and my mother to do this. Please stay safe.*

*We will.*

FINN, her father, and grandfather crouched in the shadows of the castle. "Since Frakar has already sent his invasion force, there won't be as many people around. That should help us move through the castle undetected," Finn commented in a low voice.

"What about Krakos?" Finn's grandfather asked.

Finn's father spoke up. "I saw him leave on the leviathan again when I was on my work detail today."

Finn's grandfather nodded and pointed to one of the open windows farther up the castle wall, above their heads. "I can elevate Finn up to the window, and if the room is clear, she can enter through it. From there, she'll have to avoid Frakar's guards." He looked at his granddaughter. "I don't like you going. It will be very dangerous."

Finn gazed back at her grandfather and reached over and squeezed his hand. "My *dynamis* will keep me safe, Bappa. It has to be me. And besides, I remember the layout of the castle from when I was assigned to it for a few weeks when one of the staff had taken ill." She smiled and pulled the knapsack she had brought with her off of her back and handed it to him. "Please keep this for me. We might need it." She stood on her tiptoes and kissed his cheek. "Don't worry, Bappa. I will be okay. Remember—the apple doesn't fall far from the tree."

Finn's grandfather looped the knapsack around his shoulders and smiled affectionately at his feisty granddaughter with her fiery red hair. "You are definitely right about that." He pointed at the castle wall. "We will need to get closer."

"Yes, Bappa!"

"Good. Stand still with your arms by your sides and focus on the windowsill."

The older man planted his feet and gazed intently at Finn's back. He took three deep breaths, releasing each slowly, his brow crinkled in concentration. The moonlight caught Finn's hair, causing it to glow as she slowly began to rise, her feet coming off the ground and her body moving upward. She rose to the level of the window and carefully looked inside. "It's empty, Bappa," she whispered.

"You can reach your arms out now, Finn." He muttered a few words in the ancient language to draw his *dynamis* from deep within. "I can't hold you safely much longer."

Finn reached her arms out and grabbed the sill with her hands. She swung her body over it and swiveled to the floor inside. Her red head popped out the window a moment later. "I'll see you at the service entrance."

Finn's grandfather motioned to her father, and the two men moved stealthily through the castle grounds. They approached the service entrance and waited in the shadows.

"Do you think she's okay?" Finn's father bit his lip, concern in his eyes.

"She will be fine. She has her *dynamis*," Finn's grandfather reassured the younger man. The words were barely out of his mouth when the door cracked open, and they could see Finn, grinning, gesturing them to come in.

# TWENTY-THREE

"When a plan fails, make a new plan."
~ Palar, strategist of Tolan

The banyar bird swooped in, landing smoothly on Yandin's arm. The young man stroked the bird affectionately, then lifted its leg to remove the note attached. Yandin left the bird contently eating and headed to the castle to deliver the message.

Rugal and Jackal were just finishing their breakfast in the cozy atmosphere of the library, when the young blacksmith entered and offered Rugal the note that had been affixed to the banyar bird. "This message just came in, Sire."

"Thank you, Yandin." He gestured at the table. "Have you eaten breakfast?"

Yandin bobbed his head. "Yes, Sire." He hesitated. "May I stay?"

Rugal nodded. He started to read the message, and his

expression darkened. "Our forces on the southern coast couldn't contain all of the Neliphim. Just as we were afraid of, the Neliphim have started rowing their boats up the Great River."

He turned to Jackal. "I think it's time for us to start moving. Dungellan and his swordsmen will need to stay so they can defend the castle if the Neliphim get past our forces at the Great River."

Jackal narrowed his eyes, considering Rugal's words. He rubbed his chin, weighing all of their options. He finally turned to Yandin.

"Please ask Melad for provisions for the king and six of his guardsmen. Check Tag to make sure he is travel-ready." He sighed and looked at Rugal. "I will alert Dungellan of the need. You must go, but I must stay. Someone has to be here to receive communications and coordinate our forces." He gestured toward the west. "Kalbin is where you need to go. The Neliphim are heading up the river. We must stop them there, or Cargoa will be sandwiched between the enemy forces coming from the Great River and the eastern coast, and the Neliphim will be in a position to take the castle."

He strode over to the table where the map was spread out and gestured to Rugal. The young king walked over and placed his hand with the Ring of Rosin on the map. They could see figures on horseback racing from the northwest toward Kalbin. "It looks like the Kargoliths are moving to Kalbin as well," Rugal observed. He looked at Jackal. "The Ring of Rosin said our futures are dependent on our kingdoms working together. Elayas and the Kargoliths are taking part." He ran his hand through his hair, his eyebrows drawing together. "But Tolan can't."

Jackal reached out and patted his son's back. "It will work itself out, son. Just do the best you can."

Rugal shook himself and nodded. He allowed himself to smile, despite the dire circumstances, as a thought popped into his head. Felan would be proud. The thought of running away had not crossed his mind even once. "You are right, Father. We have come too far to give up now."

LISSA COULDN'T STAND STILL, pacing the shoreline, waiting for the huge sea creature to respond to her call. Mura and the guardsmen could keep lookout for the Neliphim without her—she had to do something to help get Princess Gillian and the others back home. She waited impatiently, when finally, the water erupted in front of her, and the leviathan gazed anxiously at her.

*I heard you calling for me.*

*Yes, I need your help.*

*How can I help you?*

*You can carry me across the sea, to the lands of the Neliphim, and help me find Argothal the dragon.*

*Why?*

*We need to rescue our friends. Frakar has captured them. Argothal can help, but he needs to know about it.*

*I have no saddle for you. I am not sure you will be able to hold on.*

Lissa smiled at the concern in the sea creature's voice. *I will get my horse's saddle then. I can add extra rope to the girth so it will fit around you. Will that suffice?*

The leviathan bobbed its head. *I think so.*

*Good.*

FINN MOTIONED to her father and grandfather to follow her. The castle hallways were dark, and most of the wall sconces unlit, which worked to their advantage. They moved quickly through the castle and up a staircase.

Finn pointed to a door, "I think it likely that they could be imprisoned in there. I can sense Uncle Zander."

Finn's father walked up to the door and carefully disengaged the bar keeping it locked, sliding it back.

He winked at Finn. "Let's find out."

He slowly opened the door and stepped inside, Finn and her grandfather on his heels. The Swordsman was lying on a pallet on the floor, and Legas and Kenrik quickly rose from their chairs. Finn's father put a finger to his lips and motioned for Legas and Kenrik to help the Swordsman up. They worked quietly and quickly, holding him up on either side. The Swordsman stifled a yelp when he banged into a chair leg in their hurry to get him out. They all followed Finn back to the service entrance and out the door.

"Bring Uncle Zander back home," Finn instructed Kenrik. "We need to go back in and rescue Princess Gillian and Soldar."

Before the Swordsman could object, Kenrik ran over to where the cart they used to transport him had been left and brought it back around. "Here," he urged the Swordsman. "Get in."

The Swordsman started to protest, but noting the determined expressions on Finn's and Kenrik's faces, he blew out a breath of exasperation and complied.

Finn turned to Legas. "Do you know where Soldar and Princess Gillian are being held?" Legas nodded. "I think I know where Soldar is. I saw him looking out one of the south-facing windows when we arrived at the castle. Unfortunately, I haven't seen Princess Gillian."

Seeing the Swordsman and Kenrik headed back to the compound under cover of the night, Legas turned to Finn's father and grandfather. "You two, please wait here. I don't know what we might run into and we may need help." He turned back to Finn. "We better get going. The castle staff will begin to stir soon."

"No cause for concern," Finn grinned. "I know all of the staff. But yes, it would be best to avoid the need to provide an explanation."

Legas followed Finn's lead as she raced up the castle stairs. They came to a room on the second floor on the south side.

"This must be it," Finn whispered.

Legas strode forward and slid the heavy bar back that was keeping the occupant within trapped inside. He opened the door quietly, peering into the room.

Soldar, sparse brown hair rumpled, jumped up from the couch he had been sleeping on, fumbling for his glasses. He quickly found them and shoved them on his nose. "Who are you? What do you want?" he asked, squinting in the darkness.

Legas took a step. "We are here to rescue you," he replied in a hushed, soothing tone.

"Legas?" Soldar walked over to the man standing just inside the doorway. "It's good to see you!" The pudgy scholar noticed Finn standing behind Legas as his eyes adjusted to the dim light. "And who is this?"

Finn stepped around Legas, smiling shyly. "I am Zander's niece." Seeing Soldar's raised eyebrows, she elaborated. "The Swordsman. I am the Swordsman's niece."

Soldar smiled broadly. "How wonderful to meet you!"

Legas cleared his throat. "I'm sorry, Soldar, but we must get going. We don't want to run into Frakar."

"Of course, of course," Soldar replied, pushing his glasses farther up his nose and firmly in place. "But we must retrieve something first."

Legas and Finn exchanged glances. "Are you sure? We need to find Princess Gillian, too. We haven't much time."

"That works out well," Soldar replied. "I have become somewhat familiar with the castle environs during my stay. Frakar has been quite talkative during our many conversations. What I need to retrieve is in the same place. Unfortunately, they are both in the most secure location of the castle— the top tower."

Legas and Finn looked at each other in dismay. Legas held a hand up. "But what about Frakar?"

"His royal suite takes up the floor below the tower, directly above us. We have to pass through his floor to reach the top."

Finn's eyes sparked with determination. "I have to go."

Legas nodded his agreement, and Soldar tilted his head in question. "Her *dynamis*," Legas explained. "She can disappear for brief periods of time—long enough to prevent being discovered."

"But we will have to get Princess Gillian and the box down," Soldar's brow crinkled in consternation. "They won't be able to pass through Frakar's floor without being detected."

"Is there a window in her room?" Legas asked.

"Yes," Soldar replied. "But no way to get down from it."

"Perhaps there is a way." Finn looked at Legas and grinned. "My Bappa and my father should still be waiting for us at the castle wall. You and Soldar can make your way back to them and tell Bappa we are in need of his *dynamis* once again." She thought for a moment and added. "Be sure and ask him to bring my knapsack."

Legas and Soldar left the castle through the service entrance, striding through the shadows toward the castle wall where they could just make out two figures crouching against it. "Soldar, this is Finn's father and grandfather," Legas said in a low voice. He motioned to them, "Finn is making her way through the castle. She has to go through the level Frakar is staying on to get to the top level."

"I trust her *dynamis* will see her past Frakar's rooms," Finn's father commented, trying his best to sound confident.

"That is the plan," Legas admitted.

Finn's father lifted his eyebrows in concern. "But once she is at the top level, how will she and Princess Gillian get out?"

Legas looked at the Swordsman's father. "She said her Bappa would know what to do. She also asked that you bring her knapsack."

"She did, did she?" the older man, grizzled with age and hard labor, stared up at the stars for a moment, and smiled. "Hmmph. We shall see." He turned to the younger men. "Follow me."

The four crouched low and ran through the shadows, scurrying to the side of the castle where Soldar indicated the princess was imprisoned. The Swordsman's father pulled the knapsack off of his shoulders and peered inside, rummaging through its contents and nodding to himself.

"What is it?" Legas asked curiously.

"It's Finn's climbing kit," Finn's father replied. "Part of her job is to climb the trees in her care when they require trimming, medication, or administering nutrients." He beamed with pride. "She is very talented. Not many have her knowledge and agility."

"Talents that will be invaluable once we return home to Elayas," the Swordsman's father commented as he closed the knapsack and peered upwards at the window. Just as he expected, a red-haired figure looked out the window and waved her hand.

"Legas, if you would be so kind, stand close to the castle wall and hold the knapsack as high as you can," the Swordsman's father instructed, handing him the knapsack. "Be ready to turn it loose when you feel it tugging away from you."

Legas nodded and accepted the knapsack, holding it above his head. The Swordsman's father stepped back and focused on the knapsack, once again exerting his *dynamis*. An inanimate object of smaller size was easier to control. Legas rocked back on his heels and let go as the knapsack started to elevate. They watched as it moved upward along the side of the castle into Finn's outstretched hand. She grinned and waved, then pulled it in and went to work.

"It's easy," Finn reassured Princess Gillian as she fastened the saddle around her and attached the ropes. "All you have to do is climb out the window, and I'll lower you to the ground."

Princess Gillian looked out the window and gulped. She gave Finn a weak smile. "I guess there is no other way, is there?"

Finn smiled reassuringly at her. "No, there's not. But I have done this a hundred times. You'll be fine. I promise."

Princess Gillian nodded and clambered onto the windowsill. She took a deep breath, then following Finn's instructions, she kept her feet against the side of the castle as Finn lowered her down.

Legas reached up and grabbed her as she approached the ground, and once she was steady, Finn's father disconnected her from the saddle. Finn was peering down, and Legas gave her a thumbs up. She rapidly brought the saddle back up and affixed a carved wooden box to it. Lowering it out the window, she managed to place it on the ground. Soldar moved quickly to release it from the saddle and gave the rope a tug, signaling to Finn that it was her turn. She hauled the saddle back up and, with a big grin, came flying down the side of the castle.

# CHAPTER
# TWENTY-FOUR

"Your past does not define you or your future."
~ King Johan of Kargolith

"What is it?" Rohan anxiously waited for his brother to read the note the banyar bird had just delivered to the Kargolith camp. One of the Kargoliths took the bird to its resting place and gave it fresh food and water.

Johan stood in the midst of the camp, and everyone gathered around.

*The Neliphim are rowing some of their fleet north up the Great River. Our estimated head count is that there are six hundred Neliphim on twelve ships. We must stop them before the Kalbin junction of the river, or they could invade to the east and capture Cargoa. Without Tolan's archers, only the Kargoliths stand between the coming evil and their progression to the king of Elayas' castle. They must be stopped.*

Johan's heart dropped in his chest. He looked around at the small but determined band of Kargoliths surrounding him. Since they had to split their troops when Tolan was forced to withdraw, he did not have the sheer numbers needed to stop the oncoming invasion. They were also a long distance from Kalbin. Not knowing where and when the invasion would happen had been costly to their plans. He paused to think. The only way to achieve what must be done would be by using *dynamis*. He needed someone with a *dynamis* that could stop the Neliphim ships from traveling up the river. An idea started to form, and he looked about, searching for the dark-haired head of Rohan's friend. "Elgibran!"

The young man was standing back in the crowd and, at the sound of his name, moved forward, making his way to the leader of the Kargoliths. He stopped a few feet away. "Yes, Johan?"

Johan took a deep breath, then let it out. "We do not have enough fighters to do what King Rugal is asking. You mentioned your *dynamis*. You are able to transport objects through the air?"

"Yes, he can!" Rohan jumped up and down with excitement, interrupting his friend, who was about to speak. "I've seen it myself. Elgibran can transport objects with his mind."

Johan held up a quieting hand toward his brother, then turned back to Elgibran. "Can you use your *dynamis* to build a blockade across a raging river? Something to prevent the Neliphim schooners from moving forward?"

Elgibran looked down and rubbed the toe of his boot in the dirt in front of him. He didn't look Johan in the eye, and his voice trembled. "I can't."

Johan gazed at Elgibran and then looked at Rohan, eyes

raised in question. Rohan shrugged and walked over to Elgibran, and put an arm around his shoulder. He returned Johan's gaze as Elgibran continued to look down.

"Elgibran lost his brother, when he was unable to prevent a rockslide from coming down on him. He had not been trained at the Sepharim school yet."

Johan looked at Elgibran with compassion. "I understand your reluctance, Elgibran, but your past does not define you or your future. You can do this."

Elgibran shook his head, still staring at the ground. Johan pursed his lips, thinking, then came to a decision. "If you agree to do this, Elgibran, Raksh is yours."

At Johan's words, Elgibran looked up in astonishment. "Raksh?" he whispered.

Johan nodded, his heart hurting but knowing he was doing what he must. He could sense Elgibran just needed a push, and Raksh was that push. He had a feeling it could change not only the course of the invasion, but also profoundly impact Elgibran's life for the good. "Yes. If you will use your *dynamis* to help us blockade the coming ships, Raksh is yours."

Elgibran nodded hesitantly, and Johan smiled. He turned to Rohan, whose eyes were slightly glazed in shock at Johan's sacrifice. "Come, Rohan. We must get the men organized and on our way. We haven't much time."

Rohan nodded, slapped his friend on the back, and began organizing the men who had gathered around to hear the message.

Elgibran walked as if in a daze and joined the group who were packing their saddle bags and mounting their horses. His hands shook as he accepted the reins of Raksh from one of the Kargolith youths in charge of the herd. Johan mounted a paint horse named Lakosh, half-brother to Rohan's gelding Jakash, and the Kargoliths started making their way toward Kalbin at a fast clip.

Soldar clutched the box to his chest as they ran through the fields surrounding the castle, streaks of sunlight shining in the eastern sky. Princess Gillian was right behind him, Legas, Finn's father, and grandfather, bringing up the rear, with Finn in the lead. Running toward the compound, Finn came to an abrupt stop, staring in the direction of the sea. Everyone slid to a halt, breathing hard and looking in the direction Finn was pointing. A leviathan was headed toward the beach, a figure in a saddle on its back. The creature was moving rapidly through the waves, its bluish-grey scales almost indiscernible in the water. It propelled forward onto the beach and lowered its head, allowing the person in the saddle to climb down and onto the shore.

"Thank you, Shernolgar," Lissa reached out and stroked the giant creature's fins on its enormous face. "Could you please wait?" She gestured up the beach. "I may need another favor."

Shernolgar bobbed his head in response and backed away gently, easing into the deeper water of the harbor. He remained there, his head partially submerged but with his eyes still above water, watching. Lissa spotted the group of people coming down the path and waved. Princess Gillian, recognizing Lissa, gave a little shriek of joy and started running toward her. Lissa began to run as well and the two friends met on the beach, embracing.

"I am so glad you are okay!" Lissa exclaimed. She reached out and stroked Princess Gillian's cheek, reassuring herself that the princess was unharmed.

Princess Gillian smiled in return. "I am fine, Lissa. I took an unexpected detour on my trip to meet Yandin, but I am no worse for wear." Her face clouded. "Frakar kept me imprisoned in a room in the castle, but he did not harm me."

"That is good news, indeed," Lissa replied. She looked past Princess Gillian and spotted Soldar, still holding onto the box. "Soldar! It is good to see you." She reached out and touched his wrist. "Mura was so worried. We all were. I will send word to Rugal, so everyone knows you are okay."

Soldar bobbed his head. "That would be outstanding, Lissa. But may I ask, how did you traverse here on that leviathan? I thought Frakar had entrapped its mind."

Lissa smiled. True to form, Soldar was always curious. "You are correct, Soldar." Her expression saddened. "Frakar has indeed entrapped a leviathan—this one's mate. She even now is being ridden by Krakos who is spearheading the Neliphim invasion." She gestured toward the sea. "Shernolgar is her mate. Frakar cannot entrap two minds at once. It is an enormous drain of his *dynamis*. Shernolgar remains free, mourning his mate's imprisonment."

"Wait..." Finn interrupted. "How do you know this?"

Lissa laughed. "I am still learning about the potential of my *dynamis*. Not only can I speak to Rugal across great distances and Argothal across short ones, but I can also speak to Shernolgar. He told me."

Finn's eyes widened in awe. Lissa reached out and gave her a hug, then gestured toward Finn's father and grandfather. "May I ask who you are?"

"They are my father and grandfather," Finn piped up. "Zander's father."

"Ohhhhh...." Lissa's eyes lit up, and the Swordsman's father found himself being embraced by the future queen of Elayas. "We love the Swordsm...Zander." She stepped back. "It is so nice to meet you." She smiled at Finn's father and shook his hand.

Lissa glanced at Legas and recognized the Sepharim master, who often crossed paths with Rugal and Tonar. "It is good to see you all safe." Her eyebrows crinkled. "But what of Kenrik and the Swordsman?"

"They are awaiting us in the compound where we live. Frakar's guards never come inside. They are safe there."

"Very good," Lissa nodded. She glanced about. "It's getting light. Shouldn't we go there to hide and decide what to do next? I need to speak with Rugal so he can send a banyar bird to King Hamideh, letting him know Princess Gillian is safe. That will also allow Hamideh to send his archers to help."

"My brother didn't send Tolan forces to help stop the invasion?" Princess Gillian gasped.

"Of course not," Lissa replied, reaching out and putting her arm around the young woman's shoulders. "Wouldn't you leave ninety-nine to go in search of one? You are precious. We couldn't allow you to be harmed."

Princess Gillian smiled through the tears flowing freely down her cheek. "Please let Rugal know I am safe as soon as you can."

Lissa nodded. "We'd better go."

"There's one more thing, Lissa." Soldar blocked their path. "I have to get this box to Rugal as soon as possible." He cleared his throat and stared anxiously at Lissa over the top of the lid. "I am not at liberty to explain, but our ability to repel the invasion may depend on it."

"But how can you get it to him?" Finn looked from Lissa to Soldar.

"I have an idea," Soldar replied. He took a deep breath and blew it out. "I arrived here against my will on his mate. Do you think Shernolgar will take me back?"

"I had a feeling there may be a need for quick transport back to Elayas. I asked him to wait. Let me ask him if he is willing. Leviathans have their own magic. He can return you to Elayas in just half a day."

Soldar nodded. "Yes, about the time it took for me to travel here. I was hoping so."

Lissa stared toward the sea while the others stood quietly. Finally, she turned to Soldar and winked. "You best get going. Your ride awaits."

A thought struck him. "What about everyone else?" Soldar asked.

Lissa grinned. "I have another friend that must be around here somewhere. I think we'll be fine." She pointed at the sea creature who had come up the beach again. "Shernolgar is waiting for you."

Soldar smiled at the group standing in the sand and, clutching the box, trotted toward the sea. The leviathan ducked his head and Soldar met his gaze and nodded in return. He clambered into the saddle, being careful not to drop the box. He wrapped his arms securely around it, then firmly grasped the saddle's handles. The sea creature reared its head upward and swiveled around, propelling its coils out toward the sea. In just moments, they were a fleck on the horizon and a moment more, no longer in sight.

The sun was becoming more visible. Lissa turned to the others. "Come. Please show me to the compound. I must contact Rugal about Princess Gillian. We will need all of the help we can get."

# TWENTY-FIVE

"Leviathans are guardians of the sea; they can be your greatest
friend or your worst enemy."
~ Wanlan, Arlesian Shipmaster

Rugal sat in his saddle, circling Tag in an effort to calm him as the big bay responded to his mood and the brisk morning air. Suddenly, he felt Lissa's presence in his mind. It felt urgent, and he stroked Tag's neck while trying to listen to what Lissa had to say.

*Rugal! I am in the land of the Neliphim. I rode the leviathan here.*

*What!?* Rugal's mental voice conveyed his shock and worry. *Why did you do that?*

*I had to do something,* she replied, making her mental tone as soothing as possible. *I have good news. I am here with Legas, Finn, Kenrik, the Swordsman, and Princess Gillian. We are all safe in the compound where the people from the Swordsman's village are kept. The Neliphim don't know we are here—most of them are gone across the sea to take part in the invasion.*

*That is wonderful news!* Rugal began to breathe more easily and Tag, sensing his rider releasing his tension, also calmed down.

*Rugal, that means you can tell King Hamideh that his sister is safe. He can send his archers to help repel the Neliphim!*

Rugal let out a cheer, and Jackal and Yandin looked at him in question. Rugal brought Tag closer to where they were standing and leaned down with a huge smile. "Lissa rode the leviathan she befriended to the lands of the Neliphim. Princess Gillian is safe! The Swordsman's party is also safe!"

Jackal grinned and turned to Yandin, "Please get a banyar bird ready. We must send a message to King Hamideh and direct the Tolan archers to the eastern coast, where the Neliphim were seen at Beacon 11E. The message we received this morning said fighting is heavy there. The Arlesian fleet has engaged the Neliphim ships. Archers will have a distinct advantage in stopping the Neliphim troops. They can prevent Cargoa from being sandwiched between the Neliphim forces coming from the south and the east."

"Yes, Jackal!" Yandin almost skipped with joy. Princess Gillian was safe, and the Tolan archers were joining the fight!

Rugal breathed a sigh of relief and smiled at Jackal. "You were right. The three kingdoms are working together after all!"

*One more thing, dearest,* Lissa's sweet voice continued. *Soldar is riding the leviathan back to Elayas. He said he has something very important he must get to you. He said it will aid you in your fight against the Neliphim.*

Tag was dancing around again, eager to be off, and it was getting hard for Rugal to concentrate. *Do you know what it is?* His mental voice was both curious and anxious.

*I don't, but you will know in due time. The leviathan has its own magic—it will arrive on our southern shore in just four hours. He will then travel up the Great River to find you. He did say one thing, which is very important. You must bring the Key of Power with you to battle.*

Rugal nodded, even though Lissa couldn't see him, and he patted his tunic. *I have a special place made for it in all of my tunics. It's better than having it sewn into the sheath of the Sword of Fate like the Swordsman had done for my journey to find the Ring of Rosin, although I am very grateful for his foresight. This way, I can reach it more easily, and I won't lose it like I did when I was battling Oldag.* He tapped the sheath of his sword and glanced at the Ring of Rosin on his finger. *I want all of the symbols of office for the king of Elayas available to battle the Neliphim.*

*Be careful, my love.* Lissa tried to keep the anxiety she was feeling out of her mental voice. *I will contact Argothal for a ride back for the rest of us. He has been in the northern lands of the Neliphim, and no one has seen him. I will make contact with him and arrange our transportation back.* She didn't mention the additional people including not only Finn's family, but the rest of the villagers that needed to be brought back home. She needed to figure out a way to do that, but Rugal was much too busy to add that to his plate. *Be safe, my love.*

*Yes, dearest, and you, also.*

Rugal smiled at his father. "Soldar is on his way to Elayas on the back of the leviathan. Lissa is going to contact Argothal and bring everyone home." Jackal patted Rugal's leg. "That is indeed good news." His brow crinkled. "I wonder why Soldar would risk riding the sea creature?"

"Lissa didn't know why, just that it was very important."

Jackal sighed. "I guess we'll just have to wait to find out." He looked up at his son. "Soldar is very smart. I am sure whatever he is doing, it will be helpful."

"I sure hope so," Rugal replied, a note of uncertainty in his voice. He gazed back at the man he had come to love and respect over the last several months.

Jackal smiled reassuringly at his son. "Keep believing in yourself, Rugal. We believe in you."

Rugal nodded, his eyes suddenly moist. He leaned over and squeezed Jackal's hand, then gripping the reins, he moved Tag toward the direction that would bring them to Kalbin. Three guardsmen moved to the front and three guardsmen fell in behind.

Jackal stood watching as they quickly disappeared into the trees that bordered the courtyard, pride, affection, and concern warring in his emotions. Legas' map would be useless now that Rugal was leaving with the Ring of Rosin. He would have to trust in the banyar bird communication network they had set up. He sighed. He preferred to be a man of action, but someone had to stay at the castle, ready to organize its defense if the enemy broke through. He looked about, feeling the emptiness. He sighed again. He would just have to trust that it was all going to be okay. The oracle said the future was cloudy, but as Rugal pointed out, at least the three kingdoms were working together now.

Shivering, Soldar clung to the leviathan as it propelled itself through the sea. He marveled at its magic, as it skimmed the ocean waves with incredible speed and arrived at their destination. Coming up to the southern beach where the Great River emptied into the sea, he looked at the wreckage of ships and what must be scattered wood from the beacon's windbreak. Gazing about from the sea creature's neck, he spotted a lone figure on a horse waving at him.

"Please wait a moment," he spoke to the leviathan, hoping it understood. The leviathan bobbed its head and came to a halt. The figure approached the giant sea creature, a bird perched on his shoulder. His horse started to spook as they got nearer. Soldar squinted and could see it was a young man who looked vaguely familiar. It also looked like Rugal's flutebird was with him.

"Soldar!" the young man called out. "It is good to see you! Treble just arrived with a message that Rugal received the news of your rescue, and that a leviathan was bringing you back to Elayas. I am Tonar's cousin, Fandel. I am a Patriotes and have been tasked with seeing you safely to Cargoa."

"Do you know where Rugal is now?" Soldar called out urgently.

"The Neliphim are making their way up the Great River. He is riding to Kalbin, where he hopes to stop the Neliphim."

Soldar's voice rose an octave. "We have to get a message to him! Can Treble find him?"

"Oh yes," Fandel replied. He paused to calm his horse who was shaking at the close proximity of the sea creature. "Tonar told me Treble is very good at finding Rugal. They have a special bond."

"Please send a message. Tell Rugal he must meet me in Selba, at the river. I have something I must get to him before he confronts the Neliphim." He clutched the wooden box tighter. "The outcome of the battle may rest upon what I have to share! He must meet me as quickly as possible!"

The sun was reflecting off of the water, and Fandel, shading his eyes, nodded. "I will!"

"Good. I must continue on the leviathan. Stay safe, Fandel. Until we meet again." The pudgy scholar pushed his glasses back into place, took a deep breath, and leaned forward. "I'm ready!"

The sea creature dipped its head once toward Fandel, then propelled itself toward the Great River. In moments, Soldar and the leviathan were out of sight. Fandel dismounted and reached into his saddle bags for paper to write a note. He affixed it to Treble's leg, stroked the flutebird's head affectionately, and then raised his arm. "Find Rugal, Treble."

The bird looked at him with his inquisitive eyes, then walked along Fandel's arm. He gave a chirp and leapt into the air, soon disappearing into the clouds.

*Argothal! Can you hear me?!*

Lissa sat in the hut that housed Finn and her family. It was quite crowded now that Legas, Kenrik, and the Swordsman were also inside. The Swordsman's mother cleaned and bandaged his wound while Finn's father stirred a pot of stew over a fire.

"We'll get you fixed up and some hot food in your belly," she reassured her son. She patted his arm. "Get some rest. The wound wasn't too deep and should heal well."

The Swordsman smiled up at his mother and closed his eyes, allowing himself to drift asleep.

*Argothal?!* Lissa tried again.

*I am here.*

Lissa sighed with relief. She glanced at Legas and nodded.

*Good! Thank you for answering. Are you okay? We were worried about you.*

*I am well. I have been visiting my relatives.*

Lissa could almost hear the smile in his voice.

*I didn't know I had any.*

Lissa's eyebrows shot up in astonishment.

*There are other dragons?*

*Oh, yes. At least one hundred. Maybe more. I have never been very good at counting.*

*And they are your relatives?*

*Not all of them. But some of them.*

*How did you find them?*

*I flew north to stay out of sight of the Neliphim while the Swordsman and the other humans went on their mission. I got hungry so I went in search of food, when I noticed some mountains to the northeast. They looked similar to where Ethiod and I lived in Elayas. I flew to investigate, and as I entered the mountain range, I was surrounded by dragons. They welcomed me.*

Lissa could definitely hear the smile in his voice.

*How wonderful! Where did they come from?*

*When Oldag came into power, he was afraid of dragon-kind and ordered dragons to be killed on sight. I was able to hide in the mountains with Ethiod. Other dragons fled across the sea. These are the dragons that fled and their offspring.*

*Aren't they worried about the Neliphim?*

*The Neliphim are evil. They stay far away from them. The Neliphim do not venture to the mountains.*

Lissa nodded, even though Argothal couldn't see her. She sat thinking about what Argothal had said. *Have you eaten?* she asked, her mental voice colored with concern.

*Yes, Lissa.*

*Good.* She allowed the thought tickling her mind to fully form. *You said there are around one hundred of you?*

*As much as I can tell.*

Lissa turned in her chair and spoke out loud, directing her question to Finn's father. "How many people are enslaved by the Neliphim and live here in the compound?"

Finn's father's eyebrows crinkled in thought. "About eighty people, I would say."

*I have an idea.*

Lissa leaned forward in her chair and outlined her plan to the huge dragon who had brought the Swordsman and his party across the sea.

Argothal paused and considered his reply. *I will ask.*

# TWENTY-SIX

"A horse is the most valiant of creatures and the most loyal."
~ Segin, Master Horseman of Elayas

Rugal and his guardsmen sat around a campfire, eating their travel rations and preparing to sleep. Their horses were staked out nearby, grazing and dozing after the long day's ride. Rugal stood up and brushed the dirt from his leggings. He was looking around for a good place to spread out his bedroll, when Treble came winging through the trees and flew to him, barreling into his chest. Rugal laughed, wrapping his arms around his feathered friend, supporting him. His laughter turned to concern as he noted Treble's exhaustion. He looked at the message affixed to Treble's leg. Treble gave an urgent chirp, and Rugal removed the message and gently put Treble on a tree branch. He unfurled the message.

*Greetings, Sire! Soldar has instructed me to tell you that it is most urgent for you to ride to Selba as fast as you possibly can. The Neliphim invaders must be well past the tributary to Selba by now, possibly already approaching Kalbin. Soldar is riding a sea creature, and it is moving at an incredibly fast pace up the river. Soldar has something he must give you before you confront the Neliphim. He is carrying a wooden box, which he believes the outcome of the battle may rest upon. You must meet Soldar as quickly as possible! Fandel*

Rugal let his hand, holding the note, drop back to his side. He turned to look at his guardsmen, still sitting around the fire. His gaze turned toward the grassy field where Tag was standing peacefully. The big bay horse's head was dropped, and one rear leg cocked, a sure sign that he was relaxing. Rugal then looked up at the night sky, at the moon. He reminded himself that it was the same moon Lissa could see, even across the ocean. Somehow, that was comforting. He held the paper back up and sighed. He knew what he had to do.

"Tag," Rugal called out, accompanying it with a low whistle. The big bay's head popped up, and he swung it toward Rugal, regarding him with his intelligent, liquid brown eyes. Rugal walked to his favorite horse and reached up to scratch his withers, while Tag nuzzled his arm. He strode to where they had piled their tack for the night and located Tag's saddle and bridle, with the big bay following him. He reached down and swung the saddle in place, and Tag lowered his head for the bridle. Rugal paused to check the saddlebags for provisions, made sure the Sword of Fate was in its sheath and affixed to the saddle, felt the Key of Power securely in his tunic, and glanced at his finger where the Ring of Rosin softly glowed in response to his movement. He swung his leg over Tag's back.

His guardsmen were alert, waiting for him to address them, puzzled looks on their faces. He gazed with affection at these men who had dedicated their lives to his safety and to the safety of the kingdom of Elayas.

Rugal cleared his throat. "I must ride immediately to Selba. Soldar has returned, and he has sent an urgent message for me to meet him there."

The guardsmen began to stir, some getting to their feet and looking toward their horses, but Rugal shook his head. "I have to move fast, and Tag is much faster than any of your mounts. I can't wait for you. I must do this alone."

"But Sire, we must accompany you. You will need our protection!" cried one of the guardsmen, alarm in his eyes. The others stood, nodding their agreement.

"I have *dynamis*," he reminded them firmly. "I can defend myself." He pointed to Treble, resting on the tree branch. "Please take care of Treble. He needs to eat and rest. Return to the castle in the morning. I will meet you there after I have completed my mission."

Rugal's tone brooked no argument. The guardsman did not look pleased but held to his training. "Yes, Sire."

Rugal's tone softened, and he smiled in return. "Do not worry, Tag is valiant, and he will take care of me." The big muscular bay shook his head up and down as if in agreement. "I must go now. Return to the castle after you have rested; you may be needed."

With those words, he turned Tag in the direction of Selba. He leaned forward. "Let's go, Tag!"

The big bay leapt forward, his excellent night vision finding a path through the trees. Rugal tried to relax in the saddle. They had several hours of riding time to get to Selba.

Elgibran on Raksh, Johan on his new paint, Lakosh, and Rohan on Jakash slowed their horses to a walk. The small band of Kargoliths riding behind them slowed as well. They had skirted the mountains and were getting close to Kalbin. Rohan turned in his saddle and signaled to the men behind him to be careful not to make the enemy aware of their presence. "We are nearing the Great River. Kalbin is on the other side. We must hold the Neliphim here when they arrive, or Cargoa will be attacked, and King Rugal's castle will be vulnerable."

Johan looked about for something they would be able to place across the body of water. "We need something that can be transported by Elgibran across the river," he commented, eyes searching the rocky terrain that adjoined the woods northwest of them. His eyebrows crinkled in thought. "Something strong enough to halt any ships that come against it."

His eyes fell on the leather girth that was holding Rohan's saddle to his horse. Made of strong animal hide, the wide strap encircled the horse's underbelly, holding the saddle in place.

"We can use our saddle girths!" the Kargolith king called out, excitement in his voice. He pointed to a flat area on their left. "Come," he turned Lokash toward it. "We must dismount and unhook our girths from our saddles. We can hook the girths together to make a strong rope that Elgibran can cast across the water with his *dynamis*." He grinned. "We can leave our saddles and horses here. I can hear the river just ahead. Our horses' girths strung across it will stop the Neliphim ships from going any further upriver!"

The other Kargoliths stared incredulously at their leader as if he had lost his mind. One of them stood up in his stirrups. "How can that help? The river is wide with crashing waves. We won't be able to cross it to secure a rope made of horse girths to the other side."

Rohan turned Jakash and rode up to them. "We need to

stop the ships that will be arriving from the south, traveling upriver. My friend Elgibran," Rohan pointed at the young man riding Raksh, "has *dynamis*. Once we create a rope of our horses' girths, we can secure our end to a tree on this side of the river. He will be able to string it across the river and secure it to a tree on the other side, using his *dynamis*."

The rest of the Kargoliths still looked doubtful but followed Johan's instructions. Working together, they soon had a makeshift rope consisting of their horses' girths strung together and coiled neatly.

Rohan picked it up and hefted it, then smiled at Johan. "Looks like this is exactly what we need to stop those ships!"

RUGAL PULLED TAG TO A STOP. The horse's sides were heaving, and his whole body was trembling. His head dropped as his over-exertion overwhelmed his body. The big bay had run valiantly all night. Rugal jumped off, loosening his girth and removing his saddle. He tore off part of his tunic and dipped it into the Selba river, then returned to Tag. He squeezed the fabric so that water dripped in his hands and put them under Tag's mouth, but the horse's lip just drooped; he wouldn't drink. Rugal took the piece of fabric and began gently sponging him down. Tag nuzzled Rugal, then dropped to his knees and rolled to his side. He closed his eyes, and his breath became shallow. Rugal frantically rubbed him, grasping his neck, trying to urge him up. Finally, the big horse let out a sigh, closed his eyes, and the rise and fall of his chest stopped.

"No, Tag, no," Rugal cried, gripping his full black mane and burying his face into Tag's neck. "Don't go, Tag!!"

Rugal lay there, gripping his beloved horse for several more minutes. Finally, he sat up and wiped his eyes. "You did it, Tag," he whispered. "You got me here. You saved us."

Rugal stood up and gazing down at his equine friend, he could feel his heart squeeze with the pain of great loss. He rubbed his hand tiredly across his face. "You won't have died in vain, Tag." He looked around. Noting a path a few yards away leading east toward Selba, he gazed once more at Tag. "I am sorry, old friend. I must leave you here, to go do what we set out to do."

With that, Rugal left his beloved steed and started up the path in search of Soldar. He didn't have to go far. Tag had brought him between Selba and the junction of the Great River. He could see Soldar coming up the Selba river, astride a giant sea creature, clutching a wooden box. He quickened his pace and waved his arms. "Over here, Soldar!"

The pudgy scholar looked at Rugal, then reached down and tapped the sea creature. "Please stop. We have found the one I am looking for."

The leviathan craned its neck and peered at Rugal, then brought his head close to him, allowing Soldar to hand Rugal the box and clamber down from the saddle. He turned to the leviathan. "Please wait. I must show King Rugal what I brought in the box."

The sea creature dipped its head and lowered itself back into the river, only the top of its head and nostrils above the waterline.

"Greetings, Sire," Soldar turned to Rugal and gave a quick bow.

Rugal almost bowled the shorter man over, grabbing him for a hug. "We were worried about you!"

Soldar's face reddened, and he looked down. "It's nice to know I was missed," he mumbled. He shook himself and looked back up. "No time to be sentimental, Sire. I have something very important to share with you."

"What about the leviathan?" Rugal queried.

"He seems to understand my requests," Soldar replied. "We can't communicate very well, but Lissa can—when they are close. He is the mate of the sea creature Frakar has entrapped. She does not want to help them, but she has no choice. He is helping us in hopes of freeing her from the Neliphim's evil grip."

Rugal glanced in the direction of the leviathan and nodded. "We are fortunate we have his help." He rubbed his face and gazed at Soldar, his eyes moist. "Tag is dead. He courageously carried me here to meet you. He ran himself to death to get me here on time."

Soldar reached out and squeezed Rugal's shoulder. "I'm so sorry, Sire. I know how much Tag meant to you." He thought for a moment. "Mura sent word that the Neliphim ships have already passed the Great River—Selba junction and are continuing north toward Cargoa. We have to stop them before they get there. You must ride the leviathan!"

Rugal looked from Soldar, standing soaking wet in front of him, and back to the leviathan. "Uhhh…I don't know. I have never…"

Soldar looked at Rugal, a mischievous glint in his eye. "I recall a similar situation, when you asked me to ride a dragon so that I could come to the castle and translate a mysterious scroll." He paused and winked. "One should open one's mind to new experiences after all."

Rugal looked at the older man and sighed. "You are right, of course." He accepted the box that Soldar offered him. "So, what is in here, and how can it help?"

Soldar's expression turned serious. He pointed to the box.

"Let's set it down here," he gestured toward a large flat rock near the path.

Rugal complied, placing it carefully where Soldar indicated. Soldar pushed his glasses back in place on his nose. "Do you have the Key of Power with you?"

"Yes," Rugal reached inside his tunic and pulled it out. "I thought I might need it."

"That is great news. It saves us the time it would have taken to retrieve it. You must use the Key of Power to open the box." He looked encouragingly at Rugal. "Go ahead."

Rugal nodded, placed the key into the keyhole on the front of the box, and turned it. The lid sprang open, and five mirrors emerged, floating in the air above.

Rugal jumped back in surprise. "What are they for?"

Soldar smiled. "When you turn the key a second time, the mirrors spread out, and each one enlarges to the size of a man. You can then withdraw the key, and through your *dynamis,* you will be able to position each mirror so you can focus your *dynamis* through the Key of Power onto each mirror's surface. Your *dynamis* will bounce off each mirror and become amplified into a focal point so powerful, it can cause its target to burst into flame."

Rugal gaped and stared at Soldar. "That would allow me to destroy the Neliphim ships." His brows drew together, and he took a slight step back. "That sounds impossible."

"It's not," Soldar reassured the young monarch. "King Rosin did just that against the pirate marauders that attacked our southern shoreline many years ago."

Rugal stood a moment, absorbing Soldar's words. He finally blew out a sharp breath. "Show me."

# TWENTY-SEVEN

*Keep trying until you succeed.*
~ Tenet of the Sepharim

"Over there," Johan pointed. "See that tree on the other side?" He turned and looked intently at Elgibran.

The young man nodded, his face pale. "I can transport the girth rope across the water, but I am not sure I can tie one end around a tree." He licked his lips nervously. "I have not attempted that degree of manipulation before."

Rohan stepped up next to his friend and put his arm around his shoulders, giving him a gentle shake. "You can do it, Elgibran! I have seen you practicing and you have gotten quite accurate at placement." He stepped away. "Go ahead, try. We have this end already secured, so we can't lose the rope if you miss."

Elgibran stood at the bank of the Great River, waves

crashing below. Just as he was about to focus his *dynamis* and send the rope across the river, one of the Kargoliths Johan sent to reconnoiter came riding up at a gallop, bareback.

The Kargolith pulled up in front of them and jumped off his horse. "We can see them downriver!" he shouted. "They will be here soon!"

Johan nodded and turned back to Elgibran. "You have to do it. We won't be able to hold the Neliphim ships back if we can't secure the far end."

Elgibran nodded, his mouth gone completely dry. He licked his lips, gazed across the river at the tree on the other side that Johan had indicated, and then turned his focus to the large coil of rope made out of the girths of their horses. His eyebrows crinkling, he swung one end of the rope up into the air and started moving it past the riverbank and over the water. He made it about three-quarters of the way across, then lost his mental grip, and the end of the rope dropped into the river, the rest of the rope flailing amidst the crashing waves.

"Quick," Rohan asked one of the Kargoliths resting on a nearby log. "Come help me draw the rope back in."

The other Kargolith jumped up and ran to Rohan. They grabbed the rope near where it was tied to a tree and started pulling. The drag against it was enormous. Both young men put their body weight to bear, drawing the rope back to the bank on their side of the river.

Elgibran let out a shaky breath. "Like I told you, I can't," he threw back at Rohan.

Rohan shook his head. "I don't believe that. Try again." He thought for a moment. "This time, just imagine you are back at the Sepharim school, and you are transporting the books back to the library. Remember you had to guide them through that small window because the library was closed, and you didn't want to get in trouble for keeping them past the time you were to turn them in? You even managed to have them round a corner and position themselves in the cart the librarian pushes about. Surely, if you can do that, this is easy!"

"I was doing that to avoid a library fine, not trying to help save the world," Elgibran retorted.

"Still," Rohan pointed out, "the principle is the same."

Considering Rohan's words, Elgibran nodded and sent the rope across the river a second time. This time the rope went further before dropping into the crashing waves. Elgibran sighed. He glanced at Johan and then Raksh, as Rohan and the other Kargolith reeled in the rope a second time. He could scarcely believe Raksh belonged to him now. He knew he needed to succeed not just because of the horse, but because everyone was depending on him. He turned his attention back to the rope. This time, he closed his eyes and imagined the river crashing below. He visualized the tree Johan had selected. He took a calming breath, then focused his *dynamis* like a hand, lifting up the rope of horse girths and moving it across the river.

The rope stayed airborne, hovering at the edge of the riverbank on the other side. Elgibran's face tightened as he focused on the end of the rope. His eyebrows drew together, and he began to sweat with the mental effort he was exerting.

"It must be tight enough to hold when the ships slam into it," Johan whispered.

Elgibran gave a barely perceptible nod, sweat now pouring from his forehead and his fists clenched with effort. The Kargoliths all gathered around, watching and holding their breaths as the leather strap wound itself three times around the tree Johan indicated and securely buckled itself.

Elgibran would have fallen to the ground if Rohan wasn't standing close enough to catch him. He smiled at the cheers of the Kargoliths around him and met Johan's gaze.

The Kargolith king looked at Elgibran with pride and affection. "Well done, Elgibran. You have kept your promise, and your actions may very well help save our people." He turned to the others. "Our mission to place a barrier across the Great River to stop the Neliphim ships is successful. Thank you all for helping to make it possible. Now, all we can do is wait and be ready to fight."

THE SUN MOVED BEHIND dark clouds, and the wind began to blow, creating greyish-white caps as the river surged along its banks. Rain began to fall in sheets. The unpredictable spring weather rains chose to descend as the Neliphim ships moved northward, toward Kalbin. A leviathan, with Krakos in the saddle affixed to its back, was in the lead.

The Kargoliths lay in wait along the banks, watching the ships approach.

"There must be ten or more. They are almost to the rope!" Rohan whispered.

Johan patted his brother's arm. "Elgibran did well. It will hold," he said, forcefully shoving his doubts aside.

"I can't watch," Elgibran squeezed his eyes shut.

They held their breath as the leviathan hit the rope, jerking her back. She bellowed with the unexpected pain and writhed, backing up, almost hitting the ship behind her. The first ship came up against the rope and jerked roughly to a stop. Elgibran opened one eye and gasped in relief as the other boats came up behind the first one, hitting the rope and each other. The ships were being pitched about in the rough waves, their crews rowing frantically, trying to steer their ships around each other.

The Kargoliths let out a cheer as two ships collided, the sound of wood upon wood crashing into each other resounding across the water. The rain continued to pour, hindering their efforts, but the Neliphim ships managed to back away from the rope. Krakos was screaming orders at the ships, motioning them to keep moving forward.

"It looks like they are lining up to charge the rope and break through. There are too many of them," Johan breathed. "I don't know if the rope will hold."

Rohan poked his brother and pointed downriver. "I don't think it will have to."

Johan looked downriver and couldn't help himself; he jumped up and cheered. A second leviathan, with Rugal astride its back, was propelling itself upriver, toward the flailing ships. As the creature got closer, Johan could see that Rugal held a large wooden box. The leviathan brought Rugal directly behind the ships and came to a halt, staying perfectly still. Rugal opened the box with the Key of Power, and five objects floated out, rotating in front of the leviathan. As the Kargoliths watched in amazement, each object enlarged to a massive, mirrored surface, the size of a man. Rugal, using hand gestures, moved the box to settle on the river bank and the mirrors around the embattled ships.

"What's happening?" Elgibran asked Rohan. "Who is that?"

"It's King Rugal," Rohan responded. "I don't know what he is doing." His eyebrows crinkled. "He must be using his *dynamis*."

Johan joined the conversation. "He told me about the Key of Power. It increases the strength of his *dynamis* if it is on his person. He is holding it in his hand. It seems he is about to use it."

The three stopped talking and turned their attention to

Rugal, who was standing in the stirrups of his saddle on the sea creature's back, holding the Key of Power high in the air. Rugal pointed the key at one of the mirrors and uttered something they couldn't hear. A flash of lightning erupted from the key, striking one of the floating mirrors, and tripled in size before landing squarely in the center of the ship closest to the rope. The ship burst into flames, and they watched it disintegrate into the river. Even the water and rain were powerless against the force of combustion ignited by the lightning bolt.

In a matter of seconds, the ship and its evil crew were completely gone.

Directing the Key of Power toward another mirror, Rugal uttered something again, and lightning burst from the key to a mirror that had floated to his left. A lightning bolt sprang from the key and struck the mirror squarely, magnifying the bolt to three times its size before it made contact with another one of the ships, which exploded into a fiery ball.

The Kargoliths watched in awe as Rugal rapidly repeated his technique, annihilating all twelve of the ships and their crews, until only Krakos astride the other leviathan was left in the river. They ran along the bank, keeping their eyes glued on Rugal and the scene unfolding before them.

Rugal began to aim the Key of Power one more time toward a mirror for one final blow to take out Krakos, when the leviathan he was riding bellowed in agony, shaking its body in protest. Suddenly, he could hear Lissa's voice in his head. *You mustn't. You would destroy the leviathan's mate.*

*You are here!*

*Yes, I knew I mustn't distract you from your battle. But you must find another way. The leviathans are not evil.*

Rugal paused, considering Lissa's words. *You are right. They also have sacrificed much.* He bit his lip, looking across the choppy water surging between them. *I must go.*

Krakos was urging his sea creature forward, drawing an arrow from the quiver on his back and stringing it to his bow.

Rugal urged his sea creature forward, ignoring the mirrors but still holding the Key of Power grasped in his hand. The rain began to pour even more heavily, and the entire sky darkened, making it hard to see.

Krakos held the bow firmly, his features twisted with hate as he drew the arrow back and took aim. He released the arrow, and it sprang forward, directly at Rugal. Rugal held up the Key of Power and the tip struck it, sending the arrow tumbling into the sea. Rugal lost his grasp, and the Key of Power tumbled after the arrow, falling into the surging waves and out of sight.

Rugal looked down in horror, his hand helplessly reaching in the direction that the key disappeared. He looked back up and met Krakos' eyes. He could feel evil emanating from the Neliphim, and he looked away, gathering his thoughts. He was feeling drained from the tremendous expenditure of energy he used destroying the ships and did not have time to employ a Sepharim technique to regain his strength.

"Rugal is in trouble!" Johan shouted over the noise of the rain and crashing waves. "Rohan, can you use your *dynamis* to help?"

Rohan nodded. "I am looking for an opportunity." Before they could say anything more, Krakos loosed another arrow, this one aimed at Rugal's heart. Johan and Rohan watched, horrified as it struck Rugal's chest, and then time froze...

The Kargoliths watched from the bank as the arrow reversed itself, flying backward into Krakos' bow. The Key of Power emerged from the murky depths of the river and back into Rugal's hand. Time started moving forward again, but Krakos stayed frozen while Rugal oriented the Key of Power, using his *dynamis* to create a bolt of lightning. Krakos unfroze, and Rugal's lightning bolt struck the arrow Krakos loosed and continued forward, hitting him squarely and causing him to fall from the saddle and erupt into a fireball.

Rugal, looking slightly dazed, turned toward the Kargoliths lining the bank and raised his fist in victory. He leaned over and spoke to the leviathan, who brought him to the bank so he could dismount. He squatted next to the box and put the Key of Power into the keyhole, turning it back to its original position. The mirrors returned to their initial size and floated back into it.

The leviathan propelled itself toward the other one Krakos had been riding, and to the amazement of those watching, they twined their necks together in greeting.

*She is still entrapped, darling. But now they have hope. What happened? I could hear your thoughts, but I don't understand how it was possible.*

A huge grin spread across Rugal's face. *Johan found his dynamis—and it's extraordinary! He can reverse time! Rohan helped, too. I'll tell you more about it later.*

*Yes, dearest. We still have to deal with Frakar. Soldar did not have time to explain, but he did mention he knew Frakar at one time and that Mura and Soldar knew him from King Rosin's court. I am going to go speak to him.*

*Are you sure that's a good idea?* Rugal couldn't keep the alarm out of his voice.

*We have Argothal with us, and...so much to tell. It will be okay, love. I will contact you afterward.*

Before Rugal could protest further, he was surrounded by Johan, Rohan, Elgibran, and the rest of the Kargoliths, eager to celebrate their victory. The rain had stopped, and the sun started to come out from behind the clouds. Light had overcome the darkness.

CHAPTER

# TWENTY-EIGHT

"We are all in need of redemption. It's just more visible in some
than others."
~ Legas, Master of the Sepharim and cartographer

"Abanyar bird arrived this morning. More good news,"
Tonar smiled at everyone gathered around the large
table in the castle library. "The Arlesian ships
attacked the Neliphim ships on the northeastern coast. The
Tolan archers, led by King Hamideh himself, arrived on the
northeastern coast in time and were able to destroy the
Neliphim before they could invade. Their flaming arrows set
the Neliphim ships afire, and they are lost in the sea."

Smiles burst forth all around the table at Tonar's words.
"Very good news, indeed," Jackal agreed. "Ethiod, what of
Janar and the Sepharim at the southern beaches. Have you any
word?"

The grey-haired musician and master of the Sepharim had

arrived the day before. "As we predicted might happen, the ships invading our southern coast broke through to the Great River." He held out his hands. "While we were unable to hold them back, we did manage to destroy two of their schooners and slow them down."

"That was definitely to our advantage," Soldar piped up. "The delay you provided enabled me to return from the Neliphim lands and meet Rugal at Selba in time for him to engage them at Kalbin." He turned to Tonar. "My thanks to the Patriotes for getting me transport here."

"We were glad to be of service," Tonar replied, his shoulders held high and a gleam in his eye.

Rugal sat quietly, watching the group of people he loved and respected gathered about the table making their reports. The ride from Kalbin had been uneventful. Unable to retrieve the rope made of horse girths since the leather had been damaged by water, fire, and the stress of holding the ships back, he had managed to hold onto Johan as they rode double without a saddle to the castle. The Kargoliths were enjoying a well-deserved dinner. It was a good day, but the danger wasn't over yet.

Lissa, the Swordsman, Legas, Finn, and Kenrik had not yet returned from the lands of the Neliphim, and Frakar was still not accounted for. He recalled the words from the Ring of Rosin: *"Even so, there are no assurances. The future is cloudy."*

He wondered how Lissa's conversation with Frakar was unfolding and tried to reign in his fears. He also shoved thoughts of his beloved Tag to the back of his mind. He did not know the results of Lissa's attempt to reach Frakar yet, and it was not yet time to grieve his equine friend. It was hard to be patient when every fiber of his being wanted to release his emotions. The unwelcome thought to run crossed his mind, but he was able to crush it immediately. The old Rugal did not exist anymore. He was a new creation and would not allow himself to be dictated by his old habits.

The Swordsman insisted he should be present to protect Lissa if needed, but Lissa firmly refused.

"You must heal," she affectionately admonished the huge man. "You have a big heart, but you would be putting yourself at great risk." The Swordsman's family all chorused their agreement with Lissa, and he leaned back on the couch and blew out a noisy breath. "I will be fine," Lissa repeated. "You know Legas is more than capable."

Princess Gillian gently stroked the Swordsman's forehead. "You must rest, Zander."

The Swordsman reluctantly nodded his acquiescence. He gazed intently at his friend and Sepharim master. "Take care of her, Legas."

"Of course, Tamadar," Legas replied formally. "I will be most vigilant."

That settled, Lissa and Legas walked up the path to Frakar's castle. The courtyard was deserted, and at their knock, no one answered the door.

Legas looked at Lissa with raised eyebrows. "Perhaps we should just enter. Kenrik mentioned all of Frakar's evil minions have crossed the sea. Only the enslaved villagers are left and may possibly be hiding from Frakar's wrath now that Soldar and Princess Gillian have both escaped."

Lissa nodded. "I think you are right."

Legas reached for the handle and pushed. Much to his surprise, the castle door opened. He stepped in first, extending his senses and looking around. Something strange impinged upon his consciousness, something vaguely familiar. He turned and looked at Lissa in surprise. "Follow me. I think I know where he is."

Lissa followed the Sepharim master as he moved through the castle to the great hall. They did not see any guards or castle staff as they made their way to what must be the throne room. The doors were already open, and Legas walked in, Lissa close behind. Legas immediately noticed the tapestries adorning the walls, and his eyebrows rose. His eyes were drawn to the figure sitting on the throne. Legas stopped, his jaw dropping, and he brought his hand to his throat, trying to contain his surprise.

"Ferrous!"

The man on the throne peered back at Legas. "Another ghost from my past," he muttered loud enough for Legas and Lissa to hear. His gaze drilled into Legas. "What are you doing here?"

"I might ask the same question of you," Legas shot back. "I thought you were dead all of these years."

"So, you spoke to Soldar and got your stories straight," Ferrous sneered. He leaned forward, his fists clenching where they poked out from the red robe he was wearing.

Legas shook his head with a confused expression. "Soldar? No, we did not have any time to talk beyond him mentioning he had met Frakar in the past. Once we rescued him, he quickly took off across the sea on your leviathan's mate." He paused and turned to Lissa. "Ferrous and I were classmates at the Sepharim School in Selba before King Rosin was overthrown." He turned back to Ferrous. "I remember that school prank of yours, when you made my horse go slower, so you could win the race." His eyes flashed. "But entrapping a leviathan against her will to wage war. That is both cruel and an abuse of your *dynamis*."

Legas paused to collect his emotions. "I had no idea it was you. Soldar said something about getting the secret of the Key of Power to King Rugal in time. Where is Frakar?"

"I am he. That is the name Magdarin gave me," Ferrous thumped his chest. "Why are you here?" he demanded.

"Soldar mentioned Mura also knew you—that you had been at King Rosin's court." He held up his hands in a conciliatory gesture. "That means you are human, not an evil supernatural force like Krakos or his minions." He softened his voice. "We are here to make peace with you."

Ferrous laughed unpleasantly. "Why should I? Even now, Krakos is leading his evil minions against you. The plan that was started so many years ago by my mentor Magdarin is about to come to fruition. Elayas and her surrounding kingdoms will be mine!"

Legas shook his head. "No, Ferrous. That will never happen. Lissa also has *dynamis*. She can communicate with King Rugal. He has already defeated Krakos. Your ships have been destroyed, and your evil minions are no more."

Ferrous stared at Legas in disbelief. "I don't believe you."

"It's true. Try to communicate with the leviathan. See what she says."

Ferrous glared at Legas, then narrowed his eyes, focusing his *dynamis* to reach out to the entrapped creature. His eyes grew wide. Shocked, Ferrous stood up, his face confused. He glared at Legas. "Yet again, your actions have ruined me!"

Lissa had been standing off to the side, listening to their exchange, and chose that moment to step forward. "No Frakar, or Ferrous, or whatever name you go by. Our actions have not ruined you. They have saved you! The Ring of Rosin described Krakos, not you."

She closed her eyes and began to recite the prophecy that had been burned into all of their brains:

*He is evil beyond comprehension and possesses magic through his arrows. He and his people live across the sea. He will return and bring companions with the intent to destroy all of you.*

She opened her eyes and looked at Ferrous. "Krakos is the one with the magic arrows. He is the one who returned after he shot an arrow at King Rugal. He is the one who brought companions with him back to Elayas. Not you."

Legas reached out a hand toward Ferrous. "Come back to Elayas. Come home."

Ferrous jerked back, eyes flashing with anger. "Why should I? You and everyone I knew abandoned me. The Neliphim leader Magdarin kidnapped me for my *dynamis*, but no one came to rescue me. Why wouldn't I join his side after being betrayed by everyone I cared about?"

Eyes filled with pain, Legas walked up to within inches of Ferrous. "Not true. Right after you had gone missing, Oldag killed King Rosin, and Elayas was in chaos. When we couldn't find you, we thought you were dead. We did not know you were taken across the sea. How could we?"

He raised his arm, and Ferrous ducked backward to avoid a blow that was not coming.

"We began a tradition among the Sepharim," Legas continued. "When a beloved member of our own class at the Sepharim school loses their lives unjustly, we tattoo their name on our wrist to honor them."

Legas reached up with his other hand and tore back the sleeve on his wrist. Tattooed on the inside of his wrist were two names in the ancient language. *Ferrous and Felan.*

Ferrous' eyes widened in shock, and he fell to one knee. He looked up at Legas and began to weep. "I just wanted someone to care," he whispered. "Can you forgive me?"

Legas and Lissa came forward, and Legas offered him a

hand. Ferrous grasped it, and Legas helped him up. The two men embraced. "We are all in need of redemption," Legas whispered. "It's just more visible in some than others."

While Lissa stood watching, a familiar voice came into her head.

*We are here.*

*Where?*

*In the courtyard of Frakar's castle. The dragons have agreed to help.*

Lissa looked at Ferrous and smiled. "How would you like to ride a dragon?"

# TWENTY-NINE

"Sometimes you have to leave the familiar to start a new
adventure."
~ Felan, Master of the Sepharim, to his students

Farin burst into the dining hall. Most everyone who had traveled to the southern and eastern coasts of Elayas and along the Great River had made their way back to the castle near Cargoa. King Hamideh had arrived just that morning, eager to be reunited with his sister. He shared a table with Tonar, Johan, and Yandin, who sat nervously pushing the food around on his plate. Soldar, Janar, Ethiod, and Dungellan were at another table. Rohan, Elgibran, and the band of Kargoliths that had accompanied them to the Great River were at tables further down the hall.

The young page ran up to the table where Rugal, Mura, and Jackal were seated. He stood there breathlessly, chest heaving with his exertion and eyes wide with excitement. "Come, see, Sire!! Come out to the courtyard!"

Rugal, eyebrows raised at Farin, jumped up out of his chair. The young page turned on his heel, leading the way, and the entire hall emptied, racing after him. They ran down the main corridor leading to the castle entrance, and Farin practically ran into the doors, pushing them open. Everyone spilled out of the castle and into the courtyard. Farin pointed, and all eyes looked skyward.

"I never in my wildest dreams thought I would behold such a magnificent sight," Jackal breathed to Mura, wrapping his arm around her shoulder and drawing her close.

Dragons filled the sky, all sizes and hues. Argothal was in the lead, and they could see that Lissa, Princess Gillian, and the Swordsman were astride him. He was followed closely by another dragon close to his size but a brilliant red color with golden scales. Legas, a person they didn't recognize, and Finn and Kenrik were seated between its scales. A third dragon, this one a dark green color and slightly smaller, carried who they guessed was the rest of the Swordsman's family.

An additional twenty dragons of varying colors were flying behind them, each carrying three or four people. The great beasts circled the courtyard, waiting their turn, as Argothal and the two dragons closest to him backwinged into the court-yard grounds and landed.

Rugal raced to Argothal, who crooned as Rugal wrapped his arms about his massive jaws in a hug. Treble came winging through the courtyard, chirping wildly, landing on top of Argothal's head, spreading his wings and flapping them in excitement.

"Thank you for bringing Lissa and everyone back!" Rugal choked out. He had not realized the depth of his emotion at seeing his people safely returned. He reached up and helped

Lissa step down, and they both jumped back as Yandin propelled himself up Argothal's extended foreleg. He reached out his hand toward Princess Gillian. "May I help you down?" He managed to stutter.

Lissa and Rugal looked at each other and grinned, then turned to watch Princess Gillian accept Yandin's hand and step down from the huge dragon's foreleg, Yandin swinging her to the ground. She did not release his hand but, instead, gazed into his eyes and smiled. Beaming, Yandin looked like he would burst with happiness. The two started walking together to allow space for the others to disembark from the majestic beasts.

Lissa turned back to Rugal. "You best help the Swordsman down, my love. He is still recovering from his wound."

Rugal jerked back in surprise, eyebrows raised. "What happened?"

"He attacked Krakos in an attempt to rescue Princess Gillian and got an arrow in the thigh for his trouble." She patted Rugal's arm. "Don't worry, it is healing nicely."

Rugal nodded and stepped up onto Argothal's foreleg. He clambered to the huge beast's back and held out his hand.

*Argothal, could you possibly lower yourself to the ground, so the Swordsman can dismount more easily?* Lissa sent a silent request.

Both Rugal and the Swordsman grabbed a scale as Argothal complied. Rugal jumped off of Argothal and helped the Swordsman slide down his side.

*That was perfect! Thank you!* Lissa patted the huge nose and scratched him under the chin.

Argothal closed his eyes momentarily in enjoyment then opened them and swung his head toward Rugal, Lissa, and the Swordsman standing together.

*I must go so the others can land.*

*Thank you!* Lissa spoke in her mind, and Rugal echoed out loud.

Argothal stood back up, gathered himself, and leapt back into the sky. The other dragons had been dropping their passengers off, and happy reunions were going on around them. Everyone that had been enslaved and living in the compound had been liberated and transported on the dragons back to Elayas where they would be able to rebuild their lives in freedom. It was a day none of them would ever forget.

THAT EVENING, the Swordsman sat in one of the chairs by the fire in the library. Rugal, Lissa, Jackal, Mura, Janar, Ethiod, Legas, and Dungellan were all present at his request. The big man had his leg elevated on a footstool with a pillow under it and was sipping a mug of ale. He looked about and, noting everyone had arrived, he put down his mug and cleared his throat. "Thank you for coming."

Taking his cue, they all gathered around and focused their attention on their Tamadar.

The Swordsman looked at the faces gazing back at him, with pride and affection in his eyes for each. He looked down and rubbed his leg where the bandage covered his wound from the arrow, then looked back up. "It was a hard battle, and you all did admirably. I am grateful to be a part of such a fine group of patriots." He sat up a little straighter. "But I have decided it is time for me to step away from my roles as head of the castle guardsmen and Tamadar."

The big man ignored the gasps heard among those gathered and continued. "I will be joining my family in rebuilding our village in far northern Elayas." He smiled gently. "You are all family to me, but I have another family that needs my help now."

Jackal nodded to himself. Knowing the Swordsman, that was not unexpected.

The Swordsman looked at Rugal. "You have done well. The Sepharim thanks you for your service. Your bravery has restored Elayas to what King Rosin always meant her to be, a place where her citizens can thrive and prosper."

Rugal nodded, his eyes moist. He managed a smile. "You still owe me a dinner at the best tavern in Cargoa."

The Swordsman's eyes looked a little watery as well. "Absolutely—before I leave!"

The Swordsman gestured toward Dungellan. "I don't believe there is a more accomplished swordsman on the conti-nent." He paused with a grin. "Except for myself, of course." His face grew serious again. "I have conferred with Johan and Dungellan. The Kargoliths focus on their horsemanship, but Dungellan prefers swordsmanship. They both agree that if you are willing, it is fit and in the spirit of cooperation we desire between our kingdoms, for Dungellan to continue in his duties here as head of the castle guardsmen."

Swiveling his attention to Dungellan, Rugal gazed at the stocky warrior who had been an extraordinary force during his journey to seek the Ring of Rosin. Dungellan's character and his willingness to speak up had stood out and the Swordsman found him to be a man of integrity. "Is that your wish, Dungellan?"

The warrior stood up straight and returned Rugal's gaze firmly. "Yes, Sire. It would be my honor."

Rugal looked around at the people in the room who had become his trusted counselors over the course of the last year. Seeing their nods and smiles, confirming his own feelings, he turned back to Dungellan. "We would be honored to have you serve as head of our castle guardsmen."

A sprinkling of clapping echoed through the group and more than one slapped Dungellan on the back in congratulations. The Swordsman smiled at Dungellan. "Thank you for taking this on, my friend. I can leave in peace knowing the castle guard is in your capable hands."

The Swordsman took another breath and looked at the group. "There is the other matter, that of the selection of the new Tamadar, and the passing on of my roles and responsibilities. As you know, the current Tamadar selects the next Tamadar." He rubbed his cheek and, with a mischievous gleam in his eye, continued. "As you also know, Sepharim tradition dictates that the identity of the Tamadar is kept secret, and for good reason." His tone grew serious. "We have found that the Tamadar can be a much more effective force within the Sepharim and for Elayas if their identity is not known. Only under extreme circumstances can it be revealed."

He sighed. "As you know, I revealed my identity during our fight to overthrow Oldag. At the time, I deemed it necessary, and I stand by my decision." He smiled. "But today is a new day. We will return to the tradition of keeping their identity secret. My purpose today is simply to inform you that I am passing on the mantle of Tamadar."

The room became utterly quiet as everyone absorbed the Swordsman's pronouncements; their curiosity would not be satisfied, but it was for the best. Moments passed, and Mura stepped over to the Swordsman. She leaned in for a hug. "We will miss you, old friend."

The Swordsman looked up at her and smiled affectionately. "I will miss you, too, but I am excited about the future. I haven't seen my family for so many years, I want to make up for lost time. Finn is so much like her mother. It will be good for her to have her Uncle Zander nearby." He chuckled. "I am sure I will be constantly challenged and kept on my toes." His eyes sparkled. "Kenrik will be evaluating the forests near our village for shipbuilding. Argothal and some of his relatives have agreed to come help us rebuild." He grinned and winked at Mura. "So, I am only a dragon ride away."

Rugal jerked awake. The sea creature had visited his dreams again.

*Lissa, are you awake?*

*Yes, Dearest. Are you okay?*

*I am. I just wanted to tell you that the leviathan visited my dreams again.*

*Do you need me to meet you?* Rugal smiled at the concern in her voice.

*No. I am okay. The leviathan is no longer in pain. She told me Ferrous has released her completely. She is no longer entrapped. I just wanted to let you know.*

*What about her mate?*

*He is with her now. They are happy.* He paused. *How do you thank a sea creature? She was forced to carry Krakos, but her mate carried Soldar and me of his own free will.*

*The fact that they are together again, and she is free from her mind being ensnared, is all they really wanted. I think she reached out to thank you for making it possible. Perhaps that is thanks enough.*

Rugal nodded and lay back down on his pillow. *I think you are right.*

*Good night, my love.*

*Rest well, dearest.*

CHAPTER
# THIRTY

"That's the thing about grace. It's undeserved."
~ The Swordsman's father

The mood in the throne room was somber. The great hall was fuller than usual, as citizens of Elayas poured into the section reserved for interested parties. They were there to witness the proceedings that would determine the future of the man who had kept them enslaved for more than twenty years. Rugal sat in his royal robes, contemplating the crowd. He glanced over to where the Swordsman, Jackal, and Mura sat in their usual places. Another chair was brought up for Soldar, and he took his place alongside Mura.

*This won't be easy.*

*You'll know the right thing to do. Stay true to your heart,* Lissa's lilting voice in his head comforted him.

Farin approached in the brightly colored clothing of a royal page. He stopped before the throne and bowed. "Sire, may I bring the transgressor forward?"

Rugal almost smiled. Farin was growing up before his eyes. He nodded. "You may."

Farin retreated to the doors of the hall where Ferrous was waiting and accompanied him to the throne. Farin retreated to the side, and Ferrous stood squarely a short distance away. He didn't meet Rugal's gaze but sketched a bow. "Sire."

"Ferrous. You are accused of being an enemy of Elayas. You have been brought here today so that we can explore the truth." He glanced at Soldar and Mura. "You have friends who are highly regarded Elayas citizens that know you from the past. They have already spoken on your behalf. What would you like to add?"

The older man's shoulders slumped, and he looked down, every inch of him oozing dejection. "I can't excuse what I have done," he said in a low voice, raspy with emotion. "All I can say is that I was misguided, and I truly regret my actions. I know they have hurt many fine people." He turned and looked back hesitantly at the crowd in the audience. "I can't give you back what you've lost, but I can spend the rest of my life trying to make up for it."

The Swordsman's father stood up from where he was seated in the audience and moved forward. Many recalled he had lost a daughter due to lack of medical care in the compound. They waited breathlessly to hear what he would say. He walked up to Ferrous and looked him in the eye.

He took a measured breath. "You are not Neliphim. You have been in your own prison all of these years," the grizzled older man observed. "Of your own making, although not entirely your fault. I am inclined to offer mercy," he glanced at Rugal. "If the king will allow it."

Ferrous stared back in shock. "After all I've done..."

"That's the thing about grace," the Swordsman's father replied. "It's undeserved." He walked forward and reached out his hand, gripping Ferrous' shoulder, compassion in his eyes. "We forgive you."

Rugal watched as the two men embraced, then stood up. "Ferrous, you are free. I admonish you to live a life worthy of a citizen of Elayas and a member of the Sepharim. We will remember your evil deeds no more; they will be as far from us as the east is from the west."

"That was a beautiful ceremony, with you welcoming the villagers that were brought home and recognizing each person who participated in repelling the Neliphim. It's amazing how everyone from Tolan, Kargolith, Elayas, and even Arlesia came together. Those with and without *dynamis* all joining in," Johan commented. He grinned mischievously at Hamideh. "And I thought Princess Gillian and Yandin made a charming couple at the reception."

Hamideh rolled his eyes and sighed. "I think no one is ever good enough for one's baby sister, but I must admit, Yandin comes close." He smiled. "Don't tell them, but I do approve of the match."

Johan's eyes lit up. "That's great news!" He turned to Rugal. "And it's nice to see those amazing tapestries restored to your castle."

"They are magnificent, aren't they?" Rugal agreed. "My favorite is the battle between King Rosin and the marauders. Soldar tells me it's the same one King Rosin talked about when he shared the secret of the Key of Power with him."

"And a good thing, too," Johan beamed. "I don't know how

we would have stopped the Neliphim without you using the key and mirrors." He shook his head. "Amazing!" The three young kings sat on a bench in the courtyard, pitching rocks into the dirt.

"I don't know if I would have been able to stop Krakos if you hadn't found your *dynamis* when that arrow was about to hit me," Rugal returned. "Being able to reverse time is incredible!" He pitched another rock.

"Are you returning the banyar birds to King Nakasan?" Johan queried Hamideh, deftly changing the subject.

"Of course not," Hamideh replied. "King Nakasan hasn't offered to return Flash. Since he is keeping him, the least he can do is allow us to keep the birds I traded him for."

Johan clapped his shoulder. "I'm sorry you lost him. He is a fine horse."

"It was worth having the communications we needed to help defeat the Neliphim," Hamideh replied. He gave a little sniffle. "Although I do miss him." He raised an eyebrow. "Speaking of horses, what happened to Raksh? I noticed you are riding a paint gelding."

Johan sighed and rubbed his face. "I had to give him away. He belongs to Elgibran of the Sepharim now."

"The young man that transported the rope made of horse girths across the Great River to stop the Neliphim ships?" Rugal asked.

"He's the one. He is crazy about Raksh but very unsure of his *dynamis*. I couldn't think of any other way to stop the Neliphim ships from continuing upriver where they would be able to disembark and attack Cargoa." He slid his hand through his hair. "I gave him Raksh in exchange for his agreeing to use his *dynamis* to help us."

Rugal stared incredulously at his friend. "You know, as a

member of the Sepharim, he was duty-bound to help without you giving up your horse."

Johan blew out a noisy breath. "I know. And it still hurts. But Elgibran really needed a push. By giving him my prized horse, I was telling him I believed in him. I think he needed that—he wouldn't have been able to do it otherwise. Sometimes our mental battles are bigger than our physical ones."

Hamideh nodded. "I think we all get that." He turned to Rugal. "I'm really sorry to hear about Tag. He was a valiant steed. The finest horse I have ever met."

Johan moved over and put an arm around Rugal, who was looking down, his cheek wet with tears.

"I lost him twice," Rugal whispered. "He ran himself into lameness when we were chasing the Ring of Rosin. I was so happy when he appeared back at the castle with Tonar's mare. I vowed never to let him come to harm again. He ran himself to death to get me to Selba in time." He looked at Johan and Hamideh, and sniffled. "But it's not all about me. You lost your beloved horses as well."

Uttering those words made something click in Rugal's mind. "Wait a minute," he wiped his face with the sleeve of his tunic and closed his eyes. The words of the Ring of Rosin came to him, and he spoke them out loud:

*"Your futures are dependent on your kingdoms working together. You, Johan, and Hamideh are marked, and each of you will have to give up something you hold dear for the greater good."*

The three young men looked at each other, comprehension dawning. The words of the oracle had come to pass.

6 Months Later

"Lissa, Tonar, come on, tell me where we're going," Rugal laughed. Grabbing Lissa's hand, he pulled his wife in for a kiss. They had been married for almost three months now. Tonar had been his best man and was living in nearby Cargoa. They guided Rugal to the stable, and Lissa told him to close his eyes. Tonar went into one of the stalls and led out his black mare, a spindly-legged bay colt with a big white blaze by her side.

"Open your eyes!" Lissa and Tonar shouted at the same time. Rugal opened his eyes and gazed at the colt, who walked up to him fearlessly. Rugal slowly held out his hand, and the colt nuzzled it, his soft fur tickling Rugal's palm. He turned to Tonar and Lissa, who stood there grinning. His eyebrows crinkled in puzzlement. "He has Tag's markings."

Tonar grinned. "Do you remember last year when I was kidnapped, and Tag came up lame? How our horses found each other and came back to the castle together?"

Rugal nodded, calculating the timing, "About eleven months ago."

Lissa couldn't contain herself any longer. "Rugal, meet Tag's son." She beamed at her beloved. "He's yours!"

Rugal looked from Lissa to Tonar and back down at the colt who was nudging his leg. "Everything I have lost in my life has been restored," he whispered. "I am so grateful." He stood there, tears rolling down his face.

Lissa grabbed his hand and gave it a gentle squeeze. "Never forget the Kargolith proverb, my love. *Darkness may descend, but light shall overcome it.*"

**THE END OF BOOK THREE**

# EPILOGUE

The Lord himself goes before you and will be with you; he will never leave you nor forsake you. Do not be afraid; do not be discouraged.
—Deut 31:8

# CHARACTERS OF ELAYAS AND SURROUNDING KINGDOMS

Argothal: Dragon of the mountains; guardian of the Sword of Fate and the Ring of Rosin. Friend to King Rugal.

Bappa: Finn's affectionate name for her grandfather.

Bendar: Famous artist of Elayas.

Betzar: Castle guardsman assigned to accompany Lissa and Mura in placing signal beacons for the coming invasion.

Candar: Guardsman at King Rugal's castle.

Dendin: Young villager of Kepath.

Dobber: A family work horse beloved by the Swordsman's sister, Zayla.

Dungellan: Well-known warrior of the Kargoliths, and a

member of the Mergolith tribe that merged with the Kargoliths. He is a master swordsman.

Elgibran: A member of the Sepharim from the village of Dalben. He has the ability to transport objects through the air.

Ethiod Stargazer: A master of the Sepharim and the most famous musician in Elayas.

Ethion: Ethiod's brother and innkeeper of the Stargazer Inn in Selba.

Evil Rider at River: A Neliph, member of the Neliphim Clan, their home is across the Argonean Sea. His name is Krakos.

Fandel: Patriotes and Tonar's cousin.

Farin: Young page in King Rugal's court.

Felan: A master of the Sepharim who was Rugal's teacher until Felan was killed while defending an old man from one of Oldag's followers.

Ferrous: A member of the Sepharim who, during King Rosin's reign, disappeared and is presumed dead.

Finn: The Swordsman's niece, she is a forester enslaved by the Neliphim.

Flash: A big red horse that carried Rugal when he was seeking the Ring of Rosin. Rugal gave Flash to Hamideh, as a gift for his coronation.

Frakar: The leader of the Neliphim.

Gillian: King Hamideh's younger sister.

Hamideh: King Handerbin's son, he has ascended the throne and is king of Tolan.

Handerbin: King of Tolan, the country to the northwest of Elayas. He has stepped down but remains an advisor to his son, King Hamideh.

Hakarta: King of Tolan before King Handerbin.

Jackal: Rugal's father. His real name is Aldon, and he is chosen by the Sepharim to help lead Rugal to his destiny.

Jakash: Rohan's faithful paint horse.

Janar: A master of the Sepharim, he is Jackal's teacher and mentor.

Jardan: A shoemaker in Cargoa.

Johan of Sharvindar: He played a pivotal role in the creation of the Kargolith kingdom and is now the king of Kargolith.

Kara: An original member of King Rosin's court, she is well-versed in court etiquette.

Kelar: Villager of Regos.

Kenrik: A shipbuilder, he is enslaved by the Neliphim. He is Finn's betrothed.

Krakos: Also known as the Evil Rider at River, he is a Neliph possessing magical arrows capable of great harm. He is Frakar's second-in-command and frequently rides the leviathan Frakar has entrapped.

Krent: An evil minion of Oldag in Cargoa, known for his abuse of those weaker than he.

Lakosh: Paint horse (Jakash's half-brother) ridden by Johan, King of the Kargoliths.

Landen: Arlesian master shipbuilder kidnapped by Frakar.

Legas: Member of the Sepharim and skilled cartographer who serves as the Tamadar's contact in the village of Laran.

Lenar: A member of the Sepharim who serves as the Sepharim's representative in Farath.

Lindran: One of King Rosin's counselors.

Lissa: The daughter of Ethiod Stargazer, betrothed to Rugal.

Lona: Villager of Regos, an old woman who was a student at Selba before Oldag came to power.

Magdarin: Leader of the Neliphim before Frakar. He was Frakar's mentor.

Melad: Head steward of the castle where Rugal is king.

Meron: Master tapestry maker and Ferrous' father. His tapestries were commissioned by King Rosin, and they mysteriously disappeared from the castle toward the end of his reign.

Misteria: Lady Mura's white mare.

Mubarak: Leader in the village of Laran.

Mukatak: Arlesian diplomatic liaison to Tolan.

Mura: The wife of Jackal and the mother of Rugal, a strong and wise woman who has sacrificed much for her beliefs.

Nakasan: King of Arlesia.

Nirkut: Member of the Sepharim and the Tamadar's contact in the village of Kepath.

Oldag: The evil usurper who betrayed King Rosin to gain the throne. Although his dark powers enabled him to keep his reign secure for many years, he was ultimately defeated by Rugal.

Philaten: Tamadar before the Swordsman, and his mentor.

Raksh: Johan's horse, Raksh, is dun-colored, compact, and sturdy. He is well-known for alerting Rugal that Johan was being swept away in the river, enabling Rugal to save Johan, during their journey together to recover the Ring of Rosin.

Rohan: Member of the Kargoliths and Johan's younger brother.

Rosin: King before he was assassinated by Oldag. Rosin's rule was benevolent and prosperous.

Rugal: Reigning king of Elayas and Lissa's betrothed. Son of Jackal and Mura, he has the ability to change into more than one animal form.

Shernolgar: Leviathan (giant sea creature) and mate to the leviathan entrapped by Frakar.

Silar: Villager of Laran and nephew of Mubarak.

Soldar: A member of King Rosin's original court, he is a famous scholar, well-versed in history and law.

The Swordsman: His given name is Zander. He holds the title of Tamadar, and is the leader of the Sepharim.

The Swordsman's family: The Swordsman's father and mother, along with their daughter, Zayla, and her husband, and the Swordsman's niece, Finn.

Tag: Rugal's favorite horse, he is a big, muscular bay.

Talan: Patriotes and farmer who sacrificed much to help his community during Oldag's oppressive reign.

Tilak: Patriotes serving as a courier for the beacon signal corps.

Tonar: Rugal's friend and castle artist residing in Cargoa.

Treble: Flutebird who befriends Rugal.

Tuner: Flutebird who befriends Ethiod Stargazer.

Vanjarli: Master of the Sepharim and teacher at the Sepharim school in Selba.

Yandin: Royal blacksmith from the village of Regos. He is also in charge of the royal stables and the banyar birds used to carry messages as a reliable mode of communication throughout the continent.

Zayla: The Swordsman's sister and Finn's mother.

Zerdin: Cousin to King Hamideh of Tolan.

# TERMINOLOGY OF ELAYAS

Banyar Bird: A stocky bird with a large wingspan, native to Arlesia. They are very intelligent and possess homing instincts. They are often trained to carry messages between locations, providing communication across the continent.

Bird of the Mountains: According to an ancient fable, upon finding the Stone of Fire, the Bird of the Mountains became its caretaker. Imbued with magical properties, including the ability to make music, the Bird of the Mountains was of tremendous size and magnificent beauty.

Carved Wooden Box: Companion to the Key of Power containing mirrors with magical properties.

Day of Questioning: Occurring during the Year of Wisdom, once every ten years, this day has special significance because it is when the Time of Sun Shadow happens, enabling a rightful king, in possession of a ring made from the Stone of Fire, to ask questions. The ring will provide accurate answers to the king's questions, but only during the period of the Time of Sun Shadow.

*Dynamis*: A supernatural power (such as telepathic abilities or the ability to change to animal form) that is inherited. It is exhibited in different ways and is unique to each individual. Training by the Sepharim is important in order to be able to wield it most effectively.

Girth: A wide leather strap used to secure a saddle onto a horse's back, by attaching it to one side of the saddle and looping it around the horse's belly to the other side of the saddle. It is secured by a ring on the saddle, enabling the strap to be looped through it several times for both security and for adjusting it to the size of the horse.

Gormalins: Deadly creatures of evil that terrorized the citizens of Elayas and disappeared when Oldag was defeated.

Hashomer: Keeper of the Key. One of the select few designated by the reigning sovereign to safeguard the secret of the Key of Power.

Kargoliths: The nomadic tribe living in the unsettled territory between the kingdom of Tolan and the kingdom of Elayas.

Key of Power: Belonging to the rightful king of Elayas, it focuses and amplifies his *dynamis*, enabling it to be channeled for a long period of time without the usual fatigue that typically accompanies such effort.

Leviathan: A giant dragon-like creature that lives in the sea.

Mergoliths: Two factions make up the Kargolith tribe. One faction is also called Kargoliths, and they comprise the majority of the tribe. The lesser faction, called the Mergoliths, came into the Kargolith tribe thirty years ago when their numbers were dwindling. While coming together with the Kargoliths, the Mergoliths have also retained their separate identity, which in the past was a source of contention between the two factions.

Rite of Reciprocity: Available only during a new moon, a non-Kargolith can enter the sacred circle and request to be received as a native Kargolith. By doing so, they receive the same rights and privileges as a member of the tribe.

Sepharim: A group composed of both men and women, members follow a high code of ethics and have pledged to use their supernatural powers, known as *dynamis*, to protect the people of Elayas. Representatives of the Sepharim work closely with the king of Elayas and his court to maintain peace and forward positive initiatives in the kingdom.

Schooner: A ship that is made of wood. It is capable of being rowed or sailed and can travel across oceans and on rivers.

Patriotes: Citizens of Elayas that do not possess *dynamis* but who were devoted to overthrowing Oldag and restoring the kingdom to the rightful heir, King Rugal. Patriotes worked with the Sepharim in returning their country to the same freedoms they enjoyed under King Rosin's reign.

Ring of Rosin: Commissioned by King Rosin, it is a red diamond set in a ring of gold. It glows and hums musically when worn by the true king.

Stone of Fire: Created when the foundations of the earth were laid, it is imbued with magical powers with the intention of aiding kingdoms in ruling peaceably. The stone has the ability to recognize the true ruler of a kingdom. Another magical property it possesses is the ability to impart knowledge to the true ruler during the Day of Questioning. No one knows the extent of its powers.

Sword of Fate: The sword of the king of Elayas, its bearer has the power to command the Sepharim when it is needed.

Tamadar: The leader of the Sepharim, his identity is kept secret so as to be more effective in serving his people.

Time of Sun Shadow: Occurring during the Day of Questioning, the Time of Sun Shadow is the time that the sun is completely engulfed in shadow, so that it is as if night has fallen.

Vellaquar: The name given to the Bird of the Mountains by the Kargoliths. Flutebirds are thought to have descended from the Bird of the Mountains, retaining the ability to make music found in her offspring.

# THE LORE OF THE LEVIATHANS

*When Judgment stirs, none can flee,*
*The Leviathan's might, who rules the sea.*
*The waves obey its dreadful path,*
*The skies recoil before its wrath.*

*Yet from the depths there rose another,*
*A mate in fire, eternal lovers.*
*Two as one, their souls entwined,*
*A bond no hand could dare unbind.*

*No force may break, no spell may sever,*
*What the heavens wove, shall last forever.*
*For if one should part their fated thread,*
*Their fire shall rain, and earth be bled.*

*Now deep below in endless keep,*
*They coil and turn but do not sleep.*
*And woe to him who tempts their ire,*
*For they shall drown in wrath and fire.*

*From land to brutal ocean whims,*
    *Seafarer, beware of your sins.*
    *They lay in wait, guardians of the sea,*
    *Judging the hearts of those who flee.*

*Yet upon one who is pure in heart,*
    *The dreaded leviathan will not impart,*
    *Destruction of fire nor send its wrath.*
    *But rather seek a different path.*

# INSPIRATION FROM PAINTING

Wall painting from the Uffizi Gallery, Stanzino delle Matematiche, in Florence, Italy, showing the Greek mathematician Archimedes' mirror being used to burn Roman military ships. Painted in 1600.

# Acknowledgments

One of my most favorite parts of being an author is getting to acknowledge all of those wonderful folks who have poured into me. We go through different seasons on our life journey, and I have been supported and encouraged by many during each one. The time people took from long ago to bless me still echoes in my life today, having helped me to become who I am.

Writing a book is a huge task taking not only takes creativity, but also perseverance, sacrifice, and the ability to stay motivated even when it's hard. I am grateful for my past and my present, and for the people who have helped shape my writing career, giving me the courage to believe in myself and my calling.

My husband Phil should be included as a co-author, because Key of Power would not be the book that it is, without his hours of brainstorming story scenes, critiquing the manuscript, or spoiling me with an impromptu lunch out to refresh my writing efforts. My husband is my hero.

My son Joshua and daughter-in-love Naomi are a constant source of encouragement. If I need to bounce a plot idea off of Josh (an avid reader of fantasy and a gifted writer—I am confident you will see his books out in the world one day), or I need graphic design advice from Naomi for a book cover (she is a very talented graphic designer and illustrator), I am so blessed that they are just a phone call away.

Josh and I have created all of the maps for the *Dynamis*

series together, using the original map I drew in 1986 as our starting point—always a fun mother and son project!

I was delighted to reunite with some friends from my school days recently, and their excitement and support of my author career has been extra special: Nancy "Peanut" Richey Worth, Cindee Kaye Kirby, Sharon Buehler Pipkins, and Michele Herbst Hampton. Thank you for your friendship. It seems like yesterday, we were carefree kids with no idea of what the future might hold. You have each moved through life with grace while keeping your sense of adventure and the lives of the people around you are richer for your presence in them.

Speaking of school days, I would like to recognize a few teachers that have had a positive impact on my life, when I needed it most. My father died when I was fifteen years old. I was attending Richardson Junior High during this very difficult time. Some of my teachers are no longer with us, and I don't know where the others are, but I am confident they will all have a special crown in heaven for pouring into the lives of their students—middle grade is not easy! Ron Studdert, Norman Trout, and Melinda Thomas immediately come to mind. I am thankful for each one taking the time to minister to a teenager whose world had abruptly and unexpectedly fallen apart.

I often cite Katherine Deans Evanson in my acknowledgments because we grew up together, and she is a life-long friend, but I would be remiss not to mention her parents as well. While I know them as Mr. and Mrs. Deans (Mr. Deans is residing in his heavenly home), their names are James and Mary Ann Deans. This wonderful couple has decades of service to the children and families where I grew up in Richardson, Texas. The positive impact they have had on our community is immeasurable. Their precious granddaughter, Gillian Deans, is a real life princess to all of us, in her beauty and indomitable spirit.

The words of a song we used to sing in Girl Scouts come to mind:

*Make new friends but keep the old. One is silver and the other gold.*

I have been blessed by numerous family members and friends over the years (too many to mention them all), and I am so grateful for each one. They include: Jane Vaughn, Eddie and Susan Venetucci, Joseph Venetucci, Vincent Venetucci, Katherine Evanson, Mary Oller, Andrea Amosson, Ross Irvin, Jennifer Crippen, Amy Klingele Garman, Ashley Skoczynski, Lucy Lyons Willis, Carrie Speights, and Jan and David Swann. Family and friends truly are one of God's greatest gifts!

It takes a team to write, edit, and publish a book, and I have the best. Joseph Fredrickson is an incredible editor and has blessed me with his skills over much of my writing career. Credit for the quality of editing across all of the *Dynamis* books goes to Joey's diligence and passion for producing the best product attainable.

Beta readers provide a level of objectivity that is critical in creating a polished manuscript. Special thanks goes to Phil Golden, Barbara Taylor, Rose Randall, and Gion-Karlo for their insightful feedback, elevating Key of Power to the best reader experience possible.

I can't speak highly enough about my cover designer, Piere D'Arterie. Finding a true artist, who is willing to collaborate with me until the the vision I want to communicate in my book cover is fulfilled, is a rare find. Piere and I are both committed to not using AI in our endeavors, which enhances our working relationship. I think his work is breathtaking—each book cover in the *Dynamis* series has a beautiful continuity of imagery with the one before, which reflects his artistry.

I had the best childhood!! I grew up in a house full of love with my big brother Eddie and my mom and dad. When I was a little girl, Mom sewed our swim tags on our bathing suits when school let out, and we spent our summers swimming at Terrace pool—coming home for a bologna sandwich at lunch time, then walking back to the pool to swim or to watch a puppet show in the park. My time after school was spent crawdad fishing, riding horses, and playing flag football in the street with the other kids on our block, until it got dark. Mom would read stories of Babar the Elephant to my brother and I at bedtime. She listened patiently when I brought books home from elementary school that I was assigned to read out loud.

My chair in the family living room was located next to a lamp so I could read while everyone else watched TV. Mom would take me to the Richardson Public Library and drop me off for a couple of hours. I would come out with a stack of books higher than my head, carrying them to the car as she waited patiently. When I continued to read under my blanket with a flashlight past bedtime, she pretended not to see me. My love for reading has sustained me through some of the most difficult times of my life, and I am grateful to my mom for instilling it in me from a very young age.

I must also acknowledge you, dear reader, for you are the reason I write. I am so grateful to my Lord and Savior Jesus Christ for the calling on my life to write stories that overcome the darkness, and I pray that they impact you in a positive way, uplifting you and pointing you toward the light.

# About the Author

Nancy Golden wears a lot of different hats—She is a wife and mom, author, engineer, professor, horsewoman, and small business owner. She is a follower of Jesus Christ. She is a member of the National Space Society and also the founder of a writing group—the Carrollton League of Writers.

Nancy lives in a suburb of Dallas, Texas and loves to ride bicycles and horses. She has been a Trekkie for as long as she can remember and always wanted to ride a dragon.

Catch up on Nancy's latest writing endeavors and other fun stuff at nancygoldenbooks.com

I had a wonderful time writing the *Dynamis* trilogy, and I am very excited to share my stories with you. Key of Power is the climax of the series and while each book can be read on its own, I think you'll have a lot of fun following the journeys of the characters by reading all three. Sword of Fate will provide some great backstories for many of the characters you meet. Ring of Rosin continues Rugal's adventures with mysterious allies as he embarks on a perilous quest to recover the Ring of Rosin.

I hope you enjoy reading my books! If you do, please

recommend them to your family and friends. Teachers may also want to consider them for their classroom libraries and can visit my website to download a free curriculum guide for Sword of Fate.

Being an author is hard work, but it is also a joy. My heart's desire is for the words I write to have a positive impact on my readers and brighten their day—that is my wish for you. You can email me directly at nancy@goldencrossranch.com with any comments. I would love to hear from you!

*One of the best things you can do for any author is leave a review—I hope you'll consider doing so.*

# ALSO BY NANCY GOLDEN